HOME TOURS, HISTORY & HOMICIDE

A Dogwood Springs Cozy Mystery

SALLY BAYLESS

Paperback ISBN: 978-1-946034-26-7

Kimberlin Belle Publishing LLC

Contact: admin@kimberlinbelle.com

Publisher's Note: This is a work of fiction. Names, characters, places, and incidents are a product of the author's imagination. Locales and public names are sometimes used for atmospheric purposes. Any resemblance to actual people, living or dead, or to businesses, companies, events, institutions, or locales is completely coincidental.

Cover art by DLR Cover Designs, www.dlrcoverdesigns.com.

Chapter One

Monday, Oct. 23

IF I DIDN'T KNOW BETTER, I'd think the repairman was about to tell me he'd found a dead body buried in the museum's basement.

He shifted his weight from one foot to the other. He took off his ball cap, scraped a hand through his thinning hair, and put the cap back on. And all the while, he kept his eyes fixed on my office floor.

Finally, I couldn't take any more stalling. "So, how long will it take to repair the furnace?"

He took off his cap again and raised his eyes to look at me with pity. "I'm sorry, Miss Ballard. Repair isn't an option. The museum needs a whole new system."

Nerves tightened in my stomach. "A whole new system? What happened?"

"Your heat pump had multiple leaks in the coolant

lines, and they caused the compressor to seize up. When it went, the motor failed, and then the electronics fried." He cleared his throat. "It all has to be replaced."

Was there an option to go back to when he was stalling? Because as the director of the Dogwood Springs History Museum, ultimately it was up to me to keep the place running, and to be honest, a hastily buried dead body might have been easier to deal with.

We were a small, private museum in a little tourist town in southern Missouri. Our endowment helped fund the salaries for me and two other paid staff, but it wasn't set up to provide for big expenditures. A significant part of my job was fundraising to cover basic operating expenses. At the moment, we were planning a historic homes tour to raise seed money for a capital campaign to add a much-needed elevator. We weren't hoping for all the money for an elevator this year, just enough to say we'd gotten started.

I glanced across my desk at Alice VanMeter, the president of the museum's board of directors and its number one volunteer, who had been meeting with me about the homes tour.

Her eyes looked tense.

I needed an actual number from the repairman. "How much are we talking to replace the system?"

"I've got someone back at the office checking prices to be sure, and we do offer the museum a small discount because it's a nonprofit, but I'd say you're looking at around $15,000."

The knot in my stomach edged into nausea. My parents

had paid less than half that when they replaced their heat pump a year ago. Of course, the museum—a big, white Greek Revival built in 1920 as the home of a wealthy local businessman—was a lot larger and older than my parents' house. But still... "That seems awfully high."

"Well, you know, we'll have to redo wiring, replace duct work, and bring things up to code." The repairman hooked his thumbs in his back pockets, making his company shirt stretch across his broad chest, distorting the logo that said Jack's Heating and Cooling. "This is going to be a big job."

Just what I didn't want to hear.

It wasn't the repairman's fault. As I knew all too well, even if he had serviced the unit in the past and recommended replacement or preventive measures, my predecessor would have vetoed them. This wasn't the first problem I'd encountered that had been caused by her reluctance to spend money on building maintenance. Only the most expensive.

I stood, shook his hand, and gave him one of my business cards. "Thank you for coming out today. Please email me as soon as you have a firm estimate."

"Will do." He tipped his ball cap and left.

I sat back down and looked over at Alice.

Alice was about my mom's age, in her midfifties, but she dressed well and looked younger. Her teal blouse and black pants were polished and professional, and the cut of her chin-length, light brown hair flattered her face. But it was her cushioned, low black heels that told the real story. Alice was a doer, a cornerstone of the community who volunteered not only at the museum but also at the hospital, the library, the food pantry, and her church.

She was not normally thrown by obstacles, but her face looked grim. "I'd say we should get another estimate, but Jack's is the best HVAC business in town, and I know Jack personally. We won't find a better price."

Given what I'd learned of Dogwood Springs, Alice's friendship alone had probably cut $2,000 off the estimate. The woman was incredibly well connected.

But $15,000. Where were we going to get...

The reality of the situation sank in. "The museum's not going to have an elevator any time soon, is it, Alice?"

"I don't think so."

I'd had such big plans.

Currently, if you needed to go to the second floor or the third-floor attic of the museum, you had two choices—the elaborately carved walnut main staircase or the much plainer and narrower back stairs. With an elevator, we'd be able to develop display space on the second floor that was unused because of accessibility issues, and we'd make things easier for our staff and volunteers. Moving artifacts from storage on the third floor down either set of stairs could be quite a challenge.

Our goal with the homes tour was to sell 150 tickets at $35 a head for a tour of five local homes, each a distinctive architectural style from a different time period, spanning a large portion of the town's history. My colleagues at the museum, Imani and Rodney, and I had been working up scripts for the tour guides. We'd found some fascinating stories about former owners of the homes, stories that would not only entertain the visitors but also help them see the connections between themselves and the past.

The homeowners would be rewarded only with our deep praise and the chance to show off their homes, meaning that if we sold all the tickets, the day should net the museum more than $5,000. Not nearly enough for an elevator, of course, but enough for a symbolic start. Only yesterday, one of our donors agreed to pitch in $10,000 after we raised the first $5,000.

That was before the news about the HVAC system.

But dwelling on my disappointment wasn't going to solve anything. I needed to take action.

Ordinarily, I liked to psyche myself up a bit before calling a big donor, but sometimes, as director, I had to deal with crises as they arose. I looked at Alice. "I think I need to go ahead and call the man who was willing to contribute $10,000 to the elevator and see if he's willing to give that money toward the HVAC system instead. Do I need to run that by the board?"

"No. You and I are in agreement, and this is an emergency."

"Thanks."

Alice nodded and sat, twisting her hands together. She knew as well as I did that $15,000 was not in the budget. If we couldn't pivot and use the projected elevator seed money, we'd be struggling to pay our bills all winter.

I found the phone number on my computer. Then I smoothed my shoulder-length brown hair and straightened my favorite green blouse, the one that normally gave me confidence because it matched my eyes. At last I adjusted my pearls so that the clasp was in the back and dialed.

After the bad news about the HVAC system, I expected to get voice mail. Instead, the donor answered on the first ring.

Adrenaline did a jerky dance in my veins. Why hadn't I taken the time to plan out my talking points? I'd just been so flustered that I acted out of character, but there was no backing out now.

As calmly as I could, I laid out what we'd learned.

The donor listened quietly and asked what HVAC firm had given us the estimate. "Let me think for a moment," he said.

There was a long pause, during which my stomach churned, and then he agreed to switch his $10,000 donation to the furnace once we raised the first $5,000 with the homes tour.

I thanked him repeatedly, told him how much he was helping the museum, then hung up and exhaled.

Alice, who had leaned forward, listening in, sat back in her chair. "You did it. And you were amazing. That was some very persuasive talking."

"Maybe he heard the shock in my voice when I mentioned the price," I said. "I guess I knew we might one day have to replace the HVAC system, but I never dreamed it would be so expensive." In my previous position as part of a much bigger staff at a historic home in Philadelphia, I'd never given building maintenance a thought. "I'm grateful the donor was so flexible."

"I'm grateful we already had the homes tour in the works," Alice said. "It was a good idea before, but now it's essential." She pointed at the brochure mock-up on the desk. "This is such a great plan, though, that I'm pretty confident we'll be able to raise the money."

"We'll do it." I squared my shoulders. "Once we let the community know the situation, they'll be even more eager to support the tour."

"They will." Alice's eyes shone. "Goodness, I'm awfully glad you're here, Libby."

"Me too." In spite of the broken furnace, in spite of what would be a long delay in my plans for an elevator, there was nowhere else I'd rather be.

She tapped her watch. "Well, I'd better get going. I'm picking up my grandsons and taking them to our house to spend the night. It's my daughter and son-in-law's anniversary. My husband and I thought they might like a night without the twins."

"I'm sure they will appreciate it." I shut down my computer. "I guess I should head home as well. Bella will be ready to go outside."

"I'll walk out with you." Alice stood and shot a glance at the shoebox sitting on my desk. "Okay, I know it's none of my business, but why do you have a box of men's leather slippers, size 11, on your desk?"

I took my oversized purse out of the bottom desk drawer and patted the lid of the box. "I think that's the only box

Rodney had available. He put a new artifact in there, something he thinks Imani and I won't be able to identify. Tomorrow, he says I get to look inside, and I have a week to figure it out. Then I pass the box to Imani, and she has a week. If one or both of us figures out what it is, we win. If he can stump us, he says he wins."

"Does this game of Rodney's have a prize?" Alice walked out into the hall.

"Oh, yes." I turned off the lights and shut and locked the door to my office. "Bragging rights. And the loser—or losers—buy lunch at the Dogwood Café."

"You all do seem to have a good time here," Alice said as we started down the ornate walnut staircase to the first floor. "Do you think you'll be able to identify the mystery object?"

"I don't know. I normally feel confident in my knowledge of antiques, but Rodney seems sure he's going to win."

"I bet you figure it out." Alice smiled at me, said she'd use her key to lock the back door, and exited toward the parking lot behind the museum.

I left through the front door, locked it behind me and armed the security system, and then stepped out onto the sidewalk and looked back at the museum.

When I became director in early June, I viewed this museum in the small town where my mother grew up as my last resort. Not in any way where I wanted to be professionally at age thirty-two.

After my husband's infidelity, our divorce, and the way he finagled things so I lost my job back in Philadelphia, I'd come to Dogwood Springs beaten down, clinging to my belief that second chances were possible, that I could make a new life for myself.

Now, less than five months later, how things had changed. I'd found friends like Alice and my upstairs neighbor, Cleo. I'd adopted the best dog in the whole world, a lovable golden retriever named Bella. I'd met a man who—if I could release the insecurities left by my ex—I could see myself happily dating. And I'd grown to love the little town of Dogwood Springs and my role sharing its history, a history that included my own ancestors.

I gave the museum a nod of approval, shifted my purse strap higher on my shoulder, and started my walk home.

That new HVAC system would be paid for before we knew it. Because I was going to make sure the homes tour went off without a hitch.

Chapter Two

ONE OF THE wonderful things about Dogwood Springs was how close everything was, like my apartment, which was only a fifteen-minute walk from the museum.

I headed down Main Street, detouring around groups of tourists who were admiring the quaint shops, the café, the three-story library, and the upscale restaurants of downtown. The last rays of the afternoon sun illuminated the maples that lined the street, creating a warm red glow against the bright blue sky. Pots of chrysanthemums near the door of each shop coordinated with the colorful awnings that lined both sides of the street. And the sweet aroma of apple and cinnamon wafted out from the bakery and filled the air.

Eventually, I turned onto Fourth Street and followed it over to Elm, where I lived. My apartment was the first floor of a simple, white, two-story house built in 1900. The house wasn't anything fancy, but it had bits of historic character, it was easily affordable, and it was in a neighborhood filled with other older houses, lots of trees, and friendly neighbors.

Three houses away from home, I heard a familiar woof.

A moment later, Bella, my four-year-old golden retriever, galloped down the sidewalk toward me.

"Well, hello, girl." I knelt to greet her.

She wriggled around me with her tail swooshing back and forth at top speed, and when I petted her, she licked my cheek.

My heart swelled. Was there anything more wonderful than the pure, uncomplicated love of a pet? Not a day went by that I didn't realize how lucky I had been to adopt her.

The day I moved to Dogwood Springs, Bella had shown up on my doorstep. Her first owner had been the previous occupant of my apartment, a retired FBI agent who passed away. Although his daughter took Bella into her home, it hadn't worked out well, and Bella soon became mine. And what a wonderful addition she was to my life. Not only did Bella seem hardwired to show love to everyone she met, but she was also smart. Earlier in the year, when I'd been involved in investigating a murder, I was pretty sure she'd been one step ahead of me.

I gave her a pat on the back. "What are you doing out?"

She grinned at me with her tongue hanging out one side of her mouth.

I told her how much I'd missed her and carefully petted the soft fur on the top of her head, avoiding her right ear.

Before leaving for work that morning, I'd noticed her

shaking her head and rubbing that ear against the couch. From what I could tell, it was giving her some discomfort. "Don't worry, girl. I've got an appointment for you tomorrow at the vet. They'll figure out what's wrong with your ear."

"I'm so sorry, Libby." My best friend, Cleo, who lived upstairs in the house we shared, hurried toward me. "I used my key to go into your apartment to get the ladder from the basement, and when I brought it outside, Bella must have heard you coming. She darted out before I could stop her."

"No harm done," I said as we walked toward the house with Bella following behind us. Really, Bella was so well behaved that if it hadn't been for the local squirrel population, I would never have needed to use a leash. Luckily, the squirrels all seemed to be hiding at the moment.

I looked over at Cleo. "How was your Monday?"

"Great!" Cleo owned a local hair salon, and although she occasionally changed things up for a client with an emergency, she normally took off Sunday and Monday.

As you might expect, since she was the most sought-after stylist in town, her blond hair always looked good. She wore a pixie cut with long bangs and oversized glasses, and she tended to dress in bright colors. Today she wore jeans, black ankle boots, and a vivid purple sweater. She was taller than me, five feet, eight inches, to my five feet, five inches, and while I was fairly self-contained and preferred to have a plan, Cleo talked loud and fast, used lots of gestures, and withered with too much routine.

She was also a key part of my world, having welcomed me like a long-lost friend as soon as I moved in.

I pointed toward our house. "What's the ladder for?"

Cleo went to the covered front porch, bent down near two Adirondack chairs, and came out onto the lawn, holding a rather goofy-looking ghost with an electrical cord that she'd plugged into the outdoor outlet on the porch. "This!" She held the ghost by a string attached to its head and patted its face like she thought it was adorable. "The package says his name is Haunting Harold. I'm going to hang him from one of the branches up there." She gestured to the big maple in our front yard, then pressed a button at the base of Harold's neck.

His eyes lit up, and he shouted a dramatic "Boo!" After a few seconds, in a lower voice, he said "Bwa-ha-ha!" and let out a somewhat eerie "Oooooh," all about as frightening as Scooby-Doo.

Bella, who had been rolling in the grass, sat up and angled her head at Harold. She couldn't, of course, tell us her opinion, but I gathered that she wondered why we'd want such a thing in the yard.

Cleo listened to the sounds repeat on a loop a couple of times, then silenced Haunting Harold. She sat him in one of the Adirondack chairs on the porch and returned, her eyes twinkling with delight over her newest purchase.

Why was I not surprised? Every few days since late September, Cleo had added another decoration to our house. An enormous potted yellow mum, a collection of gourds, a bale of hay... Bit by bit, the place had been decorated for fall and, more recently, for Halloween.

I'd drawn the line when she mentioned the giant, hairy spiders she'd seen at the craft store. It was bad enough that I occasionally had to smash a real one with my shoe. No need to add pretend creepy-crawlies to my life.

Most of her ideas about fall décor, though, I'd easily agreed to.

I pointed toward the big, orange pumpkin that we'd bought at the local farmers' market, which now sat at the edge of the porch. "So after we put up the ghost, we'll do the carving, right?"

"That's the plan," Cleo said.

We'd agreed that today, eight days before Halloween, was carving day. That gave us plenty of time to enjoy the jack-o'-lantern but not have it rot before the big day.

"What do you think?" I asked. "A big toothy grin or a scary face?"

Cleo gave me a look that could only be interpreted as pity. "Really? We can do better than that, can't we?"

I wasn't sure what could be better than a big, toothy grin, but clearly, she had something in mind. "I, uh, I guess. Just a minute." I went inside, changed into jeans and a T-shirt, and returned to the porch.

"Here." Cleo held out her phone, which she had open to a Pinterest board she'd titled "Halloween Decor." On it, she'd collected images of pumpkins artistically carved with flowers, words, fall leaves, and one that even had the silhouette of the head of a golden retriever.

My eyes widened. "I'll scoop the insides," I said. When it came to the crafty part of the process, I needed to leave the job to her.

"Sounds good," Cleo said. "I'll get my tools."

An hour later, Cleo and I sat in the Adirondack chairs on the porch. In the distance, I could hear a kid bouncing a basketball, and occasionally, a car went up or down Elm, but in general, the street was quiet.

Bella lay stretched out on the concrete between us. Her head rested on my shoe, and she gazed up at me every now and then as if reassuring herself I was home for the evening.

After three attempts to get the perfect position, Haunting Harold had been hung from the maple tree. Cleo even scrounged through her Christmas decorations and found a timer she connected to his power cord. Starting tomorrow, from six thirty until eight thirty each evening, our house at 406 South Elm Street would officially be haunted.

A pumpkin carved with the image of a bee landing on a sunflower sat at the edge of the porch near the sidewalk. Thank goodness I'd left the carving to Cleo. She'd gone way beyond my skill level, removing only the top layer of the pumpkin when she carved and leaving a thin layer of flesh still visible in the design. "It will keep better that way," she said. "And it will glow beautifully."

"It really is a work of art," I said. And, despite my initial skepticism, I was pretty sure Haunting Harold would be a favorite of young and old alike. He hit what I thought was the perfect Halloween spot—lightly spooky, but incapable of scaring even the youngest of children. "You've made the house look great."

"Thanks." She settled back in her chair. "I love decorating for holidays. Besides, we can leave most of these decorations up until Thanksgiving. I want the place to look extra nice for when your parents visit a week from Saturday."

"Oh, that's sweet." She was such a considerate friend. "My mom will definitely be impressed."

Cleo surveyed her decorations and gave them a satisfied smile. "Your parents are only in town the one night?"

"Yep. They'll go on their vacation out west and stop back by again on their way home. Both times, they're staying at the Hilltop Bed and Breakfast. You know, the one run by my mom's high school friend, Faye Burke?"

"Sure, I know it. We've got so many great B & Bs here in town, but that one is especially nice."

I agreed. I had stayed there when I came into town for my job interview. Of course, Mom and Dad could have slept in my bed while I used the couch, but Mom wanted to see Faye and support her business.

Cleo rubbed Bella's back. "I hope they have a fantastic visit."

"Me too. Although I'm a little nervous about that Saturday night."

As if sensing my tension, Bella got up and laid her head on my knee.

Cleo looked over at me. "The three of you are having dinner with Sam, right?"

"Yeah." Much to my surprise, Sam Collins, a tech genius who'd made a fortune in California, then retired at forty to teach computer science at the local university, had asked me out two months ago. We'd been dating ever since. "It's way too soon for the whole meet-the-parents routine, but everyone—Sam, Mom, and Dad—seemed to take it for granted that we'd eat together."

"I'm sure it will be fine," Cleo said. "If they're not worked up about it, you shouldn't be either."

"You're probably right." Mom did have a tendency to be too eager to share her rather blunt opinions, but hopefully, she would be on her best behavior.

"If nothing else, you all can talk about that Clayton Smithton painting that Sam found at Ashlington," Cleo said. "And what you've learned about it so far."

I nodded. Some couples went on hiking dates, some went to concerts. Oh, Sam and I had typical dates like dinner out, but we also spent some of our time together trying to solve a historical mystery.

Two years ago, before I moved to Dogwood Springs, Sam had bought Ashlington, a house originally built by my ancestors, from one of my aunts. When he explored the attic, he found a valuable painting by a well-known American artist.

The work was a portrait of a family that we identified as

Blanche and Horace Whitfield and their daughter, Florence. When the painting was restored, we learned that another daughter, Ivy, had originally been in the portrait. For reasons we had yet to figure out, a later, lesser artist had painted her out of the portrait, covering her entire body with a window.

A light breeze ruffled Cleo's hair, and she ran a hand through it, smoothing it back into position. "I still think it's incredible that a painting worth a quarter of a million dollars was found in an attic here in Dogwood Springs."

"Yeah, that part might get a little awkward. Let's hope my mother remembers that even after the sale of Ashlington was final, Sam offered to give the painting to my aunt."

When my aunt refused to accept it, he'd paid for the restoration and donated the painting to the history museum, where it brought in a steady stream of art-lovers. He'd even paid for the new security system.

"If your mother mentions the money from the painting, just elbow her under the table," Cleo said. "But I bet she won't, especially if you keep the conversation focused on the mystery about Ivy."

"You're probably right. After all, Mom's the one who taught me to love mysteries on PBS. And maybe by the time my parents arrive, Sam and I will have found another clue."

Bella thumped her tail as if she agreed.

I exhaled and told myself not to worry.

Chapter Three

THE NEXT MORNING, as soon as Bella came back inside after a quick trip to the backyard, she scratched her ear again.

"Come here, girl." I got out a flashlight and sat down on the couch.

She trotted over.

"I'm going to look inside." I clicked on the flashlight and carefully lifted her big, soft floppy ear.

She let out a soft whine.

My heart twisted, and I gently laid down her ear. "I'm so sorry." The last thing I wanted was to hurt her. "You poor thing. I saw some redness in there." Thank goodness I'd made an appointment for her today.

I rubbed her back and told her how much I loved her.

Her big brown eyes shone.

I added a spoonful of wet food to her normal breakfast

of dry kibble, and before I left for work, I gave her two doggy treats to nibble on.

I got to the museum before nine and found the official estimate from Jack's Heating and Cooling waiting in my inbox. It was only $50 shy of $15,000.

As soon as Rodney, the curator, and Imani, the education coordinator, arrived, I called them into the first-floor conference room.

Once they were seated, I broke the news to them about the HVAC system.

"I was afraid of that." Rodney ran a hand through his short gray hair. "If only your predecessor hadn't been so darned cheap. We should have focused on raising the money to replace that unit instead of pouring money into repairs."

"I'm sorry this is going to delay the fundraising for the elevator." Imani, who was eight months pregnant, squeezed my arm, then pulled her box braids around the back of her neck and over one shoulder. "I know you really want to be able to use that display space on the second floor."

"I do. I also want us to have a way to get to our offices if we can't handle stairs." I didn't want to mention it, but before Rodney's recent knee replacement, he had often worked in the conference room instead of going up the stairs to his office. "What if I fall and break my ankle?"

A look of appreciation flashed through Rodney's eyes.

"I'm not giving up on the elevator," I said. "But first we need to make the homes tour a hit so we can raise money for the HVAC system." I pulled my sweater closer around my shoulders. "That doesn't mean you both need to work here all day, turning into ice cubes. We can mostly work from home and take shifts here for the next few days."

They looked at each other, then turned back to me and shook their heads.

"We're staying," Imani said. "What if one of us was here alone helping a guest and another guest wanted to buy something from the museum gift shop? Or what if someone stopped in to buy a ticket and no one was at the desk to sell it?"

"I want us to sell every ticket we have available," Rodney said. "Not just because we need to raise the money, but because we've got a great historic homes tour planned."

We did. First up on the list was a one-story midcentury modern with the low roofline, clean lines, and minimalist design so typical of the period. Then, a darling one-and-a-half story 1925 Craftsman owned by a nurse and a local construction worker who had poured hours of time into restoring the home. It had even been written up in a magazine as an excellent example of a Craftsman that had been modernized while respecting the initial design elements.

Next on the list was a large, elaborate Italianate home from the late 1800s, followed by Sam's house, Ashlington, a Queen Anne-style home.

And, finally, perhaps the most unusual home on the tour, at least to tourists from out of state, was a 1930s Giraffe house. Popularized by the University of Missouri Extension Service during the Great Depression, the Giraffe house building style had allowed people in Missouri, Oklahoma, and Arkansas to use available resources—large, flat slabs of local sandstone—connected with wide swaths of mortar to build the walls of their homes. From the outside, those sandstone slabs looked like the spots on a giraffe.

Rodney, who had said something to Imani that I didn't catch, stood up. "I'm going to go up in the attic and bring down the space heater for Imani's office."

"That's sweet of you," she said. "But I'll be fine. Honestly, being pregnant makes me hot, not cold."

"I'm still bringing it down, just in case." He left the room, and we heard his footsteps go up the main stairs.

"Such a sweet man," Imani said, and then her eyes narrowed. "Ooh! I've got an idea. I'm going to commission a girlfriend of mine to sell tickets to the homes tour. That girl could sell ragweed bouquets in an allergy clinic." Moving a lot more slowly than Rodney, Imani rose to her feet. She rubbed her lower back and left the room.

My staff members were so wonderful. Good at their jobs, but also such great people. And I was sure, given Alice's example, that the volunteers would be just as understanding about the chilly museum, and just as eager to work even harder to make the homes tour a success.

I fixed myself a cup of hot tea and headed upstairs.

Back in my office, I peeked in the box at Rodney's mystery item and grinned.

The mystery item, which was about the size of half a large loaf of bread, had two parts. The first was a roller on a handle, sort of like a lint roller, except that it was extremely heavy, and the rolling surface was metal and had deep groves across it. The grooves of the roller fit into the second part of the mystery item, a flat piece of metal with matching grooves. With a stretch of the imagination, you could almost imagine that it was used to cut pasta.

But I knew what it really was.

I closed the lid, sent Rodney an email with my guess as to what it was, then composed an email to the board of directors, explaining about the HVAC issue.

Late that morning, I gathered everything I'd need for several hours out of the office. I was having lunch with a potential donor, speaking at a local women's club in the early afternoon, and, finally, visiting one of the homes on the tour to drop off signage the owners had requested to use to keep visitors out of areas they wished to keep private. Plus, Bella's vet visit.

My meeting with the potential donor, a retired Navy officer, seemed to go okay. To be honest, I couldn't judge the woman well. She listened, and she asked good questions, but she gave no indication of whether she would donate.

After the luncheon, I ran home to check on Bella. Her ear was still bothering her. The vet visit couldn't come soon enough.

In contrast to the retired Navy officer, the women I spoke to in the afternoon were easy to read. They thoroughly enjoyed my presentation and fed me some fabulous homemade pecan pie. Then, while I answered follow-up questions to my talk, the club treasurer sold twenty-two tickets to the homes tour for me.

By the time I'd finished at the meeting, it was nearly

three thirty, time for Bella's vet appointment. I'd scheduled myself an hour off, so I got in my car and tuned the radio to an oldies station. Maybe it was because I was a historian, but whether it was a nice piece of antique furniture or a classic song from the '70s, I liked things that had been tested by time. I cranked up "Cecilia" by Simon & Garfunkel and headed home. Once I arrived, I let Bella out in the backyard for a moment, then said the magic word, car. Two minutes later, we were on our way to see Susie Parsons at Dogwood Springs Veterinary.

Dr. Parsons examined Bella, said that, most likely, she'd gotten water in her ear, and asked if she'd gone swimming.

I nodded. About a week ago, on an unseasonably warm day, she'd run off when we were visiting Sam and come back sopping wet.

The vet cleaned the ear and showed me how to give Bella eardrops.

The drops seemed to give Bella some relief almost immediately, and Dr. Parsons told me to use them for a week and bring her back in three weeks for a checkup.

The staff at the clinic, who were well acquainted with Bella, went out of their way to talk to her, scratch her back, and tell her how brave she'd been. For a dog as extroverted as Bella, the attention was probably almost as important to her healing as the treatment.

At last, we climbed back in my car, ready to make one last drop-off for the homes tour.

～

My last stop of the day was the Italianate home from the late 1800s. It belonged to a friend of Alice's, Gail Wellston, and her husband, Karl, a local family practice doctor.

When I'd first met with them, I'd liked Gail right away. But although I was grateful that Karl wanted their home included on the tour—an idea that seemed much more his idea than hers—I had to admit I didn't like the man.

Normally, I found family practice doctors to be practical and unassuming, but Karl seemed to be the exception. He wasn't rude to me, but glimpses of his true personality slipped out, a personality that seemed more suited to a prima donna surgeon. And it had been clear that both the purchase of the elaborate home and the extensive work by a pricey local designer had been his ideas. Even his precisely trimmed hair and beard and gleaming cuff links screamed "notice me, I'm rich."

Gail, who handled the bookkeeping at his medical practice, was a rather plain woman with short, straight brown hair and barely visible makeup. She was soft-spoken and dressed far more simply than her husband.

Despite the arrogant vibe Karl gave off, like almost every other person in town, he had succumbed to Bella's charms. Bella had met both the Wellstons when we were downtown one day, and they had encouraged me to bring her along any time I visited.

I got out, opened her door, and clipped on her leash. "C'mon girl. No need to stay in the car."

She climbed out and sniffed at some new mulch around the annuals that lined the walkway to the front door.

The Wellstons' home, which for Dogwood Springs would be considered a mansion, was two stories, but had high ceilings, so it seemed even taller. It was white and had a low-pitched roof with a bracketed cornice topped by a tall, square tower. Every element of the property, from the columned portico around the front door to the arched windows to the landscaping, had the sheen of highly paid professional maintenance. I knew it would be a favorite on the tour.

When I'd called to say I'd be stopping by, Karl said he'd be home after four and had been eager to show me some work they'd had done in the basement. Apparently, it wasn't quite up to his standards, but he did think it was an improvement.

I led Bella up the three steps to the big arched double doorway and pressed the doorbell.

It echoed inside, and Bella stuck her nose at the edge of the door and gave a loud woof.

I shushed her. "Be good, Bella." I tugged her leash to get her to move back a bit. I didn't want her charging inside before we were invited.

But no one opened the door.

We waited on the porch for a few more minutes, and I rang the bell again, but Karl didn't answer.

"Oh, well." I tucked the signs into a wire rack near the front door. "I guess Karl got tied up at the office. Maybe some medical emergency."

We started down the stairs just as a green Subaru pulled into the driveway.

Gail rolled down the passenger side window and called out, "Did you see the basement?"

Bella and I walked down to meet her.

"Karl didn't answer," I said. "Maybe he's still at work?"

Gail's face clouded. "No, he left two hours ago and texted me after he got here. Give me a minute to park, and I'll show you the renovations. I know he'd want you to see them." She drove past us, toward the detached garage.

While we waited, I admired the flowers along the side-walk, and Bella sniffed at a toad who hopped out from the base of a shrub.

"His car's here." Gail walked up behind me. "I bet Karl is upstairs and didn't hear you."

Bella moved to Gail's side and looked up at her with a happy doggy smile.

Gail knelt for a moment, patted Bella's back, and told her that they had a koi pond in the backyard that she thought Bella would enjoy seeing.

Bella lolled her head to one side, blissful with Gail's attention.

After a moment, Gail stood and rubbed one thigh as if kneeling might have been a little painful. She walked up the steps to the porch, unlocked the front door, and called out for Karl.

"Maybe he sat down to read and fell asleep?" She turned toward the living room.

From the doorway, I scanned the room, which I remembered from when I'd first seen the house. The decor was quite elegant, done in burgundy, rose, and a rich green, with beautiful hardwood floors, a thick Persian rug, and wide, dark wooden window trim and baseboards. Two large couches sat off to the left, and a pair of rose-colored armchairs flanked a small table along the right wall. Large green draperies were open at each of the four windows. And a few tasteful fall decorations sat on a table near the entrance, along with a plate of chocolate truffles. For a half second, I glanced longingly at the plate.

Gail stepped farther into the room. "Maybe he fell asleep on the couch and—"

She let out a scream.

I hurried toward her.

At the far end of the room, an end table held a crumpled napkin, a half-empty glass, and a whiskey bottle.

And between the two couches lay Karl's crumpled body.

Chapter Four

KARL LOOKED ALMOST PEACEFUL, lying on the floor, but clearly, something was wrong.

"Call 911," Gail shouted as she rushed toward him.

I dropped my big purse on a chair near the table with the truffles and pulled out my phone. Thankfully, because of the plans for the homes tour, I knew the Wellstons' address to give to the 911 operator.

Gail, in addition to her role as a bookkeeper, must have also had some medical training, at least enough to know what to do in an emergency. She checked Karl's pulse, laid him flat on his back, and opened his airway. After leaning her head near his mouth, she began CPR.

Bella strained at her leash, eager to help, but I held her back. She'd be even less use than I would be.

For a moment, I stood there, waiting on the line with the emergency operator, wishing I'd taken a CPR class. "I'll go watch for the ambulance."

Gail gave a quick nod.

Bella and I rushed toward the door.

In my hurry, I managed to knock over my purse, spilling the contents on the floor.

I ignored it and went onto the front porch, where I stayed on the phone with the 911 operator and scanned the ends of the street.

After a few minutes, a siren wailed, and an ambulance turned onto the Wellstons' street.

I moved onto the sidewalk, waving frantically until the ambulance stopped in front of the house. I led two paramedics inside and pointed them toward the living room.

A petite, gray-haired woman poked her head in the door. She introduced herself as Linda Owens, said she lived next door and was a friend of Karl and Gail's, and wondered if she could help in any way. I gratefully led her inside.

The paramedics had taken over CPR.

Gail stood near the rose-colored armchairs, twisting her hands together.

Linda rushed to her, slipped an arm around her waist, and pulled her close.

Bella and I stopped in the doorway to the living room. If I left, it would seem rude, as if I didn't care, but I didn't know what to do with myself.

Eventually, the paramedics stopped working on Karl. One of them moved toward Gail, and the two of them spoke, their heads bent toward each other.

She let out an anguished cry, covered her face with her hands, and sobbed.

The paramedic looked over at me and shook his head.

I backed into the hall, and Linda led Gail out of the room.

Unease twisted inside me. Even though I hadn't liked Karl, seeing him dead was a shock. And I wasn't a friend of Gail's, only an acquaintance. I shouldn't be here.

I stared at my spilled purse, right in the way of the paramedics, who were gathering up their supplies. Why did I have to be so clumsy? But if I tried to pick everything up, the space would be even more crowded.

The least I could do was get Bella out of the way. I led her out to my car, got her settled, and promised her I'd be back as soon as possible.

I went back inside and found Gail and Linda in the kitchen. I quickly offered my condolences to Gail, who was still crying. Then I returned to the living room, where the paramedics were picking up wrappers and other bits of trash from their medical supplies.

"I'll just grab my purse," I said.

One of the paramedics nodded.

I scooped everything back into my bag and scurried to the front door.

Outside, an odd, hollow feeling filled my chest. What a horrible thing to have happened. Granted, I'd only talked to him a few times, but Karl Wellston had seemed so healthy.

And now he was dead.

The next day was one of those warm, sunny fall days that almost seemed to sparkle. The leaves were more colorful, the sky bluer, the temperature perfect. Given the death of Karl Wellston the previous day, it seemed wrong for it to be so beautiful.

Just before nine, I put my purse in my office, and then I met Imani and Rodney in the conference room so we could talk before the museum opened at ten. A coffee maker gurgled on the counter, filling the room with the rich scent of Rodney's favorite dark roast.

"Oh, Libby, I'm so sorry about Dr. Wellston, and especially sorry you had to find him," Imani said.

"Thank you." I sat down across from her on one side of the table, taking in her orange maternity top and brown pants. On her, being so tall, it looked elegant. A shorter pregnant woman would have looked like a pumpkin. "I feel terrible for Gail. I mean, I guess a stroke or a heart attack is always a possibility..."

"He was my primary care doctor." Rodney, who was already seated at one end of the table, pressed his lips together. "He's done so much to take care of me, always watching my blood pressure and connecting me with that top-notch orthopedic who did my knee surgery, it feels weird for him to be gone. He had to be about ten years younger than me."

Rodney was in his early sixties, and I agreed with him. I'd have guessed Karl Wellston to be fifty, maybe fifty-one. "It is a bit odd. I mean, you'd think that if he had something like heart issues, he would have been on medication to treat them."

Could it have been something other than natural causes? No, everything in the Wellstons' living room had looked normal. No gunshot residue, no murder weapon lying on the ground. The fact that foul play came to mind was simply a result of the odd events that had taken place since I moved to Dogwood Springs. Anyone who had helped catch two murderers in less than six months was bound to think of homicide.

"Medication can't fix everything, I guess," Imani said.

Rodney's ruddy face tensed. "Although I hate to say it, we need to think of the homes tour." He shifted his phone back and forth from one hand to the other. "Will Gail still want their house on the tour?"

"We have to respect her grief," I said. "She may have no interest in having people traipsing through her home so soon after Karl's death."

"What a mess." Imani laid a hand on her pregnant belly. "I feel bad enough that I'm iffy for the day of the homes tour thanks to Junior, here."

Rodney pulled out his phone, tapped it a few times, and stared at it, eyes narrowed. "The day of the tour, Saturday, Nov. 18, is still three and a half weeks away." He set his phone down and ran a hand over his jaw. "And both Gail and Karl agreed to the tour," he added slowly.

"There's a chance," Imani said, "that she would want the tour to go ahead, as a way to honor Karl."

Rodney and I exchanged glances.

"Karl was certainly very eager to show the house off," Rodney said. "He even mentioned it when I had a checkup a couple of weeks ago. So maybe..." He tipped his hands palms up, with his fingers spread wide in front of him.

"We can't count on it, though. For the time being, I don't think we can even talk with her about the tour unless she brings it up." I sat up taller. "We're going to have to leave the Wellston home out of our social media posts until we know. And redesign the handout for the day of the tour to only include four houses, just in case."

"At least we're printing it ourselves," Imani said. "So we can do that as late as possible."

We talked a little longer and agreed that, since Alice was friends with Gail, after a week, we could ask her to politely check to see if Gail still wanted to participate in the homes tour. Imani offered to come up with an alternate design for the handout. Rodney volunteered to look for additional material to add to the talks the tour guides would give at the other four houses so that those stops could be longer if necessary. And I would update the social media, for now removing all mention of the Wellston home.

I sent some additional materials to the retired Navy officer I'd had lunch with, and I spent the rest of the morning creating new graphics and scheduling social media posts. Finally, after twelve, I walked home to have lunch and feed Bella.

～

"Hey, sweetie." I opened the door to my apartment halfway, and Bella squeezed out into the entryway to circle me, her tail swishing.

I patted her back and said hello.

Her big brown eyes shone with so much love that it made the whole day better.

I went into my apartment, heated water, and started brewing a mug of my favorite tea, a nice, strong British blend. Then I took Bella out to the backyard.

While she raced about and visited her favorite tree, I sat on the cold concrete back step and watched leaves floating down. I still felt a lingering emptiness, having been at the Wellstons' when Karl's body was found, but with Bella to keep me company and a strong mug of hot tea waiting for me inside, I knew the day was going to be all right.

Yes, it was sad that Karl Wellston had died, and Gail and his patients would miss him. On my way back to the museum, I'd pop into the gift shop to buy a nice sympathy card for Gail. It was the least I could do. And it was a good way to support Sandy, the woman who owned the gift shop. She and her husband had been going through a tough time, and like the rest of Dogwood Springs, I wanted to support her.

As for the museum, the homes tour might be slightly more successful if it included the Wellston home, but many of the people we hoped to draw were tourists who would never know what they'd missed. The tour could still be interesting, especially if we added more information about the other homes and the people who had lived in them over the years.

"C'mon, girl," I said to Bella. "Let's go get you some lunch."

We went inside and I took out my tea bag, breathing in the rich, fruity aroma of a fine black tea. I had just filled Bella's food bowl and given her fresh water when someone rang my doorbell.

Alice stood outside on the doorstep.

I opened the door to the entryway and the front door of the house and motioned for her to come in.

"Imani told me you'd gone home for lunch." Alice stepped inside. "I just missed you at the museum."

"Were we supposed to be meeting?" I mentally ran through my calendar. I didn't think so. "Please, come in." I waved her toward the couch, and I sat in one of the two new-to-me armchairs I'd recently added to the room.

"No, we didn't have a meeting, but I needed to speak with you. I just got off the phone with Gail."

"Oh, how is she?" The fear that she was canceling out on the homes tour flashed through my mind, but I pushed it away. The homes tour would be fine with five houses or with four. What mattered now was the poor woman's grief.

"She's terrible." Alice let out an audible sigh. "The police think Karl Wellston was murdered."

I sank back in my chair. "Murdered?"

"Yes. Did you see a plate of chocolate truffles when you were there?"

"I did. I was tempted to eat one."

Alice's eyes widened. "They were poisoned. Laced with a fatal dose of sleeping pills."

Chapter Five

A CHILL SHOT THROUGH ME, and I inhaled sharply. Those same truffles that I'd stared at, thinking they looked so yummy, could have killed me.

"Apparently, the police found chocolate smears on Karl's hands, so they checked the candy. And worst of all" —Alice's voice rose—"Detective Harper considers Gail the chief suspect."

"Gail?" I thought back on how puzzled Gail had seemed when she learned Karl wasn't answering the door, how quickly she'd begun CPR, and how she'd sobbed when she learned he was dead. "I find it hard to believe she killed Karl."

Besides, it wasn't only my gut instinct. Gail was one of Alice's good friends. Alice seemed too smart and too socially adept to be taken in by a killer.

"According to John Harper, Gail set out the poisoned chocolate truffles and just waited for her husband to eat one and die." Alice's eyes hardened. "It's absolutely ridiculous. We've got to help her. We've got to find the real killer."

"I..." Granted, I was good at logic and puzzles, and I did have a certain tenacity that had helped me identify two murderers since I'd moved to town in June.

But both times I'd almost gotten myself killed. Did I really want to get involved in another murder case?

"Please, Libby," Alice begged. "Gail is so upset. Losing her husband is bad enough, but to be suspected of killing him? It's almost more than she can take, and she's one of my best friends."

And Alice was one of my best friends as well as the woman who had hired me and helped me solve those two earlier murders.

How could I say no?

I sat up taller. "I can't guarantee we can solve it, Alice, but I'm willing to try."

Alice and I spoke a bit longer, and I texted Cleo and her high-school-aged nephew, Zeke, who had both helped us solve the previous mysteries. I suggested including Sam in our discussion, and Alice agreed.

Sam, Cleo, and Zeke replied immediately, and we made a plan to meet at seven that evening.

Alice rested a hand on my arm. "Thank you. I can't tell you how much this means to—"

My phone rang. The caller ID said, "Dogwood Springs

Police Department." I held it up so Alice could see. "Guess I better take this."

She glared at the phone as if she'd like to give the police a piece of her mind, then waved goodbye.

I answered the call.

It was Detective Harper. He asked me to come by the police station and give a statement about yesterday's events. It wouldn't help my to-do list for the day, but I agreed to stop by before I returned to the museum. I called Imani, told her Karl had been murdered, and explained why I'd be delayed.

After I hung up, I quickly reheated my tea and stuck a container of leftover spaghetti in the microwave. With the news about Karl and the poison I could have ingested, I wasn't that excited about lunch, but I needed to eat something.

I dutifully ate my spaghetti, mentally reviewing what I'd seen at Gail and Karl's home. The plate of truffles, right there on the table as anyone entered the room. The half-empty glass of whiskey, which probably enhanced the effects of the sleeping pills. And Karl, crumpled on the Persian rug, murdered.

Granted, the man had been arrogant and probably quite annoying if you spent much time around him. But who would want to kill him?

Half an hour later, I sat across the desk from Detective John Harper, glancing nervously at the stuffed, mounted fish that decorated the beige wall behind him. The detective had been businesslike on the phone, but now his thick eyebrows, which were much darker than his salt-and-pepper buzz cut, bunched together. He glared at me with the expression of a dad who'd watched his daughter miss curfew one too many times.

"Really, Miss Ballard? Another murder victim? People in town are going to talk if you keep showing up where someone's been killed."

My spine stiffened. "I didn't kill Dr. Wellston."

"I don't think you did. You've simply been unlucky—and nosy—since you moved here. But I would be very interested to learn why you were at the Wellstons' home."

My "nosiness," as he called it, had helped stop two murderers. Besides, I wasn't really nosy. I simply wanted things to make sense.

I explained about the homes tour and how Bella and I had been there to drop off signs. "I was simply doing my job." I sat back, arms crossed over my chest, shoulders tight.

"Okay, okay, calm down. I don't think you're murdering the citizens of Dogwood Springs. But I don't want you getting killed."

I relaxed a bit.

"And I would be interested to learn your observations of the scene and of Gail." The detective flipped open a small, black notepad.

Slowly, trying to make sure I remembered every detail, I recounted what had happened, making sure to emphasize how surprised Gail had seemed that Karl didn't answer the door and how she'd tried to save him.

The detective's pen scratched across the paper, and every time I paused, he looked up, as if eager for more.

Eventually, I reached the end of my story. "Then I left, thinking it was a heart attack or something."

"Excellent, Libby. Thank you. You really are quite observant."

I sat up a little taller. Maybe he did see some value in my "nosiness" as he called it.

"What about Bella?" he said. "How did she react?"

Interesting. Detective Harper knew how smart Bella was, but I hadn't expected him to ask about her.

"Well, I didn't let Bella stay in the house that long. I took her outside and put her in my car. But when we first got there, Bella sure seemed happy to see Gail." I explained that they had met before, downtown.

The detective frowned and muttered something under his breath about being an idiot, expecting a dog to recognize a killer.

Frankly, I wouldn't put it past Bella. And Bella liked Gail. Plus, one other thing didn't make sense. "Don't you think if Gail was the killer, she'd have poisoned Karl in a more public place, so someone else could be a suspect too?"

"Or maybe she staged the whole thing so that you'd be there and tell us how innocent she looked."

"But—"

He shook his head. "You're too trusting, Libby. You need to realize that everyone is not what they appear to be." He closed his notebook. "For now, I guess I need to let you get back to the museum."

I stood.

"Which is what you need to focus on," he said. "The museum. Not this murder. I do not in any way want you getting involved and putting yourself at risk."

I gave what I hoped was a believable smile, along with the slightest of nods, and hurried out of his office.

I wasn't going to neglect the museum. I had a historic homes tour to put on.

But I believed Alice when she said Gail was innocent. Which meant somebody needed to find the real killer.

Chapter Six

AT A QUARTER of seven that evening, I had just given Bella her eardrops when footsteps clomped down the stairs from Cleo's apartment.

"Ready for a walk, Bella?" I slid on a sweater and picked up my purse.

Bella bounded into the kitchen. I heard her leash fall from its hook on the wall, and a second later she came into the living room, carrying one end in her mouth.

"Libby?" Cleo called out, and she stuck her head in the door that led from the entryway to my living room. "Oh, excellent. You're both ready. Let's go have some dessert and solve this murder."

I hooked on Bella's leash, and the three of us left for downtown. Sam, Alice, and Zeke were meeting us at the Dogwood Café to discuss the case.

Cleo had already turned on the battery-operated light in

our pumpkin, and Haunting Harold said "Boo!" as we walked out to the sidewalk.

Cleo and I chuckled and started down Elm Street, admiring the neighbors' Halloween decorations along the way.

Once we reached Main Street, the sidewalk grew more crowded as tourists wandered between the shops and restaurants. At each end of downtown, near Fifth Street by Mimi's Candies and just past First Street near the museum, the high school marching band had set up a stand selling hot apple cider, filling downtown with a sweet, spicy scent of fall, jazz, and the school fight song. As I'd come to expect in Dogwood Springs, townspeople came out to support the kids' fundraiser, some making a special trip downtown just to make a purchase. More than one driver slowed, let out a passenger to buy cider, and picked them up after they rounded the block.

Bella paused for attention from the people in line for cider, and then she, Cleo, and I continued to the Dogwood Café, where the owner, Marcus, greeted the three of us by name. He pointed to Alice and Sam, sitting at our favorite outdoor table, one in a corner of the area surrounded by a low metal fence. The umbrellas that shaded the green metal tables and chairs in summer had been put away, and some of the tables were gone as well, replaced by patio heaters. Strings of lights hung high across the space, adding a cozy glow.

Alice waved and greeted Cleo and me. "And hello to you

as well, Bella." Alice turned her chair slightly and bent down to pet Bella.

"Hi, Alice." I walked toward the chair next to Sam. "Hi, Sam."

His hair was slightly rumpled, as if he'd run a hand through it, and he wore jeans, a navy polo, and a brown leather jacket, unzipped. He stood and pulled my chair out for me.

Not just tall, dark, and handsome, but so polite. How did I ever get so lucky? I hugged him and sat down.

Alice gave Bella a final pat, and Bella laid down in the corner by the fence. I slipped her a doggy treat, and she crunched loudly.

"I wonder where—" Cleo paused and pointed. "Oh, there's Zeke."

"Had trouble finding a place to park." The lanky sixteen-year-old slid into the last seat at the table, between Alice and Cleo. His dark hair was pulled back in a ponytail, and he wore jeans, a black sweatshirt, and his typical black Converse tennis shoes. For once, he'd left his enormous backpack at home. He petted Bella, then jerked his head up as if he'd remembered something important. "Do they have any pumpkin cheesecake left?"

"We do," the server said, coming up to the table. "As well as caramel apple pie and all the regular desserts."

"Sweet. Pumpkin cheesecake for me," Zeke said. "And a large cherry Pepsi."

Cleo and I looked at each other, nodded, and said

"cheesecake" in unison. I asked for hot tea and Cleo ordered a cup of decaf.

"I shouldn't." Alice worried her lower lip. "But bring me a slice of cheesecake too. And some decaf, please."

Sam ordered the caramel apple pie and regular coffee.

The server left, and Alice dipped her head toward Cleo and me. "Enjoy that metabolism while you've got it."

"Alice, you look fabulous," Cleo said.

"That's because I normally eat salads with low-fat dressing, but thank you." She looked around the table. "And thank you all for coming and being willing to help Gail."

Cleo brushed the comment aside. "Nonsense. She's your friend. And you're our friend." She leaned in, one hand on the table. "Sue Ann, the police dispatcher, came in today for a cut and color and told me some news. Apparently, the police think the candy used to kill Karl Wellston came from Mimi's Candies." She angled her head toward Mimi's, which was only a few doors down from the café.

"Halloween is a bad time for a candy shop to be connected to a murder," Sam said.

Zeke's eyes widened. "They don't suspect Mimi, do they? I can't imagine her poisoning anyone."

"No, they don't suspect her," Cleo said. "The candy had been tampered with. Someone cut a little hole in the chocolate coating on the base of the truffles, put the ground-up sleeping pills inside, and tapped the coating back into place. If Mimi wanted to poison the candy, she could have done it before she dipped the truffles in chocolate. And—" Cleo paused, waiting until the server had distributed our drinks and dessert.

Bella started to get to her feet, but I patted her head. "Sorry girl, the cheesecake isn't for you." I slipped her another doggy treat as the server moved away.

"Get this," Cleo said. "Not all the truffles were poisoned. Only some of Karl's favorite flavor, the caramel ones with a light brown squiggle decorating the top of the chocolate coating."

"Very devious." Sam pushed up his glasses.

"Gail told me that too, that the candy was tampered with." Alice took a bite of her cheesecake, closed her eyes, and paused for a moment of appreciation. "She also told me that those caramel truffles weren't just Karl's favorite. He found them irresistible. He was even quoted in a radio ad for Mimi's Candies, saying how much he loved the caramel truffles."

"Oh." Sam sat up taller. "I remember that ad. He said his wife didn't eat the caramel ones, so he'd buy a dozen of them and suddenly find that they were gone. Then he'd realize that he was the one who ate them all."

"Gail said the caramel bothered her teeth." Alice took a sip of coffee.

I set my fork on my plate and put my napkin in my lap. "So because of that ad, anyone in town would know that those truffles would be a good way to poison Karl."

"Bummer. This isn't going to be easy," Zeke said.

Cleo's eyebrows drew together. "The thing I don't get is

this—wouldn't Karl have noticed that the truffle tasted weird or had an odd texture and spit it out?"

"I've seen you eat candy," Zeke said. "You'd notice because you try to make candy last. You'd eat a truffle in at least two bites. But I bet Karl popped one truffle in his mouth after another. And the sleeping pill was probably flavorless."

I glanced over at Zeke. Was knowledge of sleeping pills common among teenagers?

He shrugged. "We learned about it in health class. Sleeping pills can be used as a date rape drug."

Oh. I sure didn't envy teenagers today. But what Zeke said about the candy did make sense. Especially since Karl had been drinking, he might not have noticed if the flavor of one truffle seemed off.

I tasted my pumpkin cheesecake and made a mental note to order the same dessert as Zeke more often. The graham cracker crust was sweet and crunchy. The filling rich and creamy and oh-so-pumpkiny. With a dollop of whipped cream on top, it was the perfect fall dessert.

I let the bite dissolve on my tongue as I thought about the murder. "Do they think someone left the candy on the doorstep? Or maybe mailed it to Karl? Or was there any sign of forced entry?"

"Not according to Sue Ann." Cleo cut off a bite of her cheesecake and dunked it in her whipped cream. "No sign that anyone had broken in, and they didn't find any packaging."

"So whoever killed Karl had to be able to walk into the

house and leave the candy on the table." Sam looked over at Alice. "That doesn't sound very good for Gail."

"That's why she called me." Alice carefully cut her slice of cheesecake in half lengthwise and separated the two halves. "She learned something though, and she told the police, but she said she didn't think they believed her."

One of Zeke's eyebrows rose. "What?"

"Karl kept an extra key at the office, and Gail discovered"—Alice paused to make sure she had our attention—"that the key is missing."

"But all sorts of people go to see Dr. Wellston at Fairview Medical Practice," I said. "Like Rodney. There could be hundreds of suspects."

Alice shook her head. "Patients wouldn't have access to Karl's office. It's down a different hallway than the one with rooms where the doctors see patients, so he didn't keep it locked. Plus, Gail said she knows the key was in his desk drawer Monday, because she saw it when she was looking for a plastic fork. So either Karl moved it and didn't happen to tell her where he'd put it, or someone stole it the day of the murder and used it to plant the poisoned candy in their home."

Sam sat down his coffee cup. "Patients might not go down that hallway, but people who work in the office would."

Zeke's fork screeched as he scraped it across his plate, scooping up the last few crumbs of his cheesecake. He looked up sheepishly.

I glanced down at my cheesecake, which was still three-fourths there.

"Hold on." Cleo pulled her phone from her purse. "A friend of mine from high school is a receptionist at Fairview Medical. Maybe she can tell us who would go down that hallway. I mean, if someone was always in a different part of the building, they probably wouldn't even know that Dr. Wellston had a key in his desk. They'd need to have seen it."

"Ooh. Good point." I sliced off another bite of my dessert. "Between you and Cleo," I said to Alice, "you seem to know every single person in town."

"Pretty much," Alice agreed. "And luckily we have Zeke helping us too, because I may know the names of the younger people in town, but they're a whole lot more likely to talk to him." She slid her plate, with the half slice of untouched cheesecake toward Zeke and opened a palm toward it, asking if he'd like it.

In less than five seconds, he'd switched his plate with hers and scooped up a bite. "Yeah, I don't know the Wellstons. I think their kids are older and have moved away. But I bet I can find a way to help with this case."

Apparently, Cleo's friend wasn't answering. She left a message and set her phone on the table. "No luck."

"Well, Gail told me something else," Alice said. "And this, at least, Gail said the police seemed to believe. The side door of the house uses a keycode, which the housekeeper knows, and Gary and Monica Boyd know."

Zeke's brow furrowed. "Who are Gary and Monica Boyd?"

"Gary's a local contractor, and Monica's a decorator," Cleo said. "She's the one who suggested your mom put in that island with the white quartz countertop."

"Oh." Zeke plunged his straw deep into his cherry Pepsi, stirring up the cherry syrup at the bottom. "So any of the three of them could have been the killer."

"Three suspects, at least," Sam said.

Cleo's phone rang.

Alice began telling Zeke and me what she knew about the Boyds, but Cleo laid a finger over her mouth.

The rest of us stopped talking. Alice and Sam sipped their coffee, and Zeke and I ate cheesecake.

A few minutes later, Cleo hung up. "Sorry, it was hard to hear. I've got three more people we should consider as suspects. My friend said her desk gives her a perfect view, and that all these people went down that hall the day of the murder."

I set down my fork and leaned in. "Who are they?"

"Dr. Roth. There are several doctors in the practice. He's the youngest and newest, and his office is right next door to Dr. Wellston's. Amber Riley, a nurse. My friend doesn't know why she went down that hall, but she did. Twice. And the first time, she looked upset when she left."

"Both of them work with medicine," Zeke said. "They could figure out how many ground-up sleeping pills it would take to kill someone."

I hadn't even thought of that. "Who's the third suspect?"

"Cheryl Nichols," Cleo said. "She takes care of all the plants at the medical practice."

"And flowerbeds around the museum," Alice said. "I don't know if you've met her, Libby. She cuts us a real deal, and I think she's hoping we'll use her services when we replace those straggly boxwoods out front. It would be good advertising for her work, since the museum's on Main Street."

I had met Cheryl, but only to say hello. "We'll check her out, the same as the others. And for all we know, there may be more suspects. But this gives us a list of people to investigate. Cheryl, the landscaper. Dr. Roth. Amber, the nurse who was upset. Monica, the interior designer. Her husband, Gary, the contractor. And..."

"And Marla, the housekeeper," Sam said.

"Thanks," I said. "I couldn't remember her name. Plus—even though I don't think she's guilty—we have to include Gail, Karl's wife."

Alice's lips grew tight, but she nodded.

"Seven suspects," Zeke said. "Where do we start?"

"I think, as soon as it seems appropriate, we talk more with Gail," I said. "She's our best source of information, and she's the person who wanted us to investigate."

Cleo, Sam, and Zeke agreed, and Alice said she would call Gail tomorrow to see when she and I could stop by.

We left the café and lingered on the sidewalk for a moment, saying goodnight. Sam kissed me and promised to text soon, and then Cleo, Bella, and I headed home.

The five of us were on the case. If it was in our power, the right person would be brought to justice.

Chapter Seven

ON THURSDAY, Imani, Rodney, and I were busy all day at the museum, trying to keep up with a large school group that had come from Westfield, about half an hour away. I didn't have time to think about the murder investigation, much less do any sleuthing.

That evening, though, Alice called and said Gail could meet with the two of us after lunch the following day. I eagerly agreed. Since Rodney had returned to work after his knee replacement, he and Imani covered the lunch shift. I could eat a sandwich while working at my desk and take my official lunch break when we went to talk to Gail.

Just before one on Friday, I parked on the street in front of the Wellstons' home behind Alice's white SUV.

The two of us climbed the steps to the porch, and Gail opened the door before we even knocked.

"Please, come in." She waved us inside and led us into the kitchen.

As I remembered from when I'd been in the house before, the room was large, the walls painted a beautiful sunny yellow. White cabinets, white marble counters, a farmhouse sink, and a gleaming copper hood over the stove complimented the Italianate design of the house. In spite of the high-end finishes and all that white, the room looked easy to live in.

Gail gestured us to a small table. "Thank you for coming over, Libby. I really hope you can help me."

The three of us sat.

"I'm so very sorry for your loss, Gail," I said as gently as I could. "I'll do everything I can to help figure out who's responsible." I let out a silent breath, grateful that I'd found a way to avoid the words *murder* and *killed*.

"I've got a lawyer, but I keep expecting the police to arrest me at any minute." Gail pressed her lips into a thin line.

Alice laid a hand on Gail's arm. "It's okay. We're here to help you. Remember how Libby solved those two murders earlier this year."

Gail gave a jerky nod. "It was bad enough before, but this morning..." She looked away, then turned back to face us, her words coming out in a rush. "This morning I was hunting in the bathroom drawer for some concealer for these dark circles under my eyes, and I found a small plastic bag of sleeping pills."

Alice and I exchanged glances.

"I've never seen them before," Gail said emphatically. "They were not mine, and I know that they weren't Karl's."

"Are you sure?" Maybe it had been suicide. I couldn't understand why someone would poison chocolates and then eat them, but stranger things had happened.

"I'm sure," Gail said. "If Karl told me once, he told me a hundred times never to store medicine in the bathroom because the heat and humidity could make it less potent." She stood and opened a nearby kitchen drawer. "Look."

Sure enough, the drawer was full of pill bottles—vitamins, prescriptions, and over-the-counter pain killers.

"Besides," Gail added, "the pills I found weren't in a prescription bottle. They were in a small plastic bag. Karl would never do that. I only figured out what they were because I looked up the markings on the Internet."

Alice angled her head to one side. "So you think someone put the pills in your bathroom drawer?"

"They must have. To frame me." Gail overlapped the sides of her pink cardigan and crossed her arms over her chest, pinning the sides of the sweater in place. "It's only lucky that the police didn't find them when they searched the house. The bag had gotten wedged in the top of the drawer."

I studied her. It seemed a bit far-fetched to believe someone snuck in, killed Karl, and planted evidence to frame Gail. On the other hand, if Gail did kill Karl, why would she tell us about the sleeping pills?

I drew in a deep breath. "I know you're not going to like this, Gail, but you need to take those pills to the police."

"I can't."

"Gail, really, you need to," Alice said gently.

"No. I'm not saying I won't. I'm saying I can't. When I found them, I was so freaked out that I flushed the pills down the toilet and then ran outside and put the baggie in the trash can right before the garbage truck ran. Not in one of our sealed garbage bags, just loose in the trash can. That was hours ago. I'm sure that plastic baggie is buried in the local landfill by now."

A sick feeling grew in my stomach. I wanted to believe that Gail was innocent, but she'd destroyed evidence. "There might have been fingerprints on the bag from the real killer."

Gail kept her arms crossed over her chest. "This person was smart enough to get into our house when it was locked and smart enough to plant evidence to frame me. Don't you think they'd wear gloves?"

Alice tipped her head to one side, then the other, as if weighing the argument. "I have to admit"—she looked over at me—"that does make a lot of sense."

I bit my lip. I was still struggling to get past what Gail had done.

"Why don't you tell us anything you think would be helpful," Alice said. "Maybe take us through the day Karl died."

Gail squared her shoulders. "First off, Alice, I know I told you that Marla, our housekeeper, knows the keycode. But I was flustered when we talked before. I don't want to give the impression that I think she killed Karl. She's in Texas, visiting her youngest daughter, who just had a baby. And Marla's been with us for years. She couldn't be the murderer." Gail grabbed her phone, tapped the screen a few times, and showed us an image of a woman sitting on a couch and holding a baby wrapped in a blue blanket. The wall above the couch displayed a large pennant for the Dallas Cowboys.

Alice and I exchanged glances. Just because the house-keeper had worked for the Wellstons for years, I wouldn't rule her out as a suspect. On the other hand, Texas was quite a drive. If Marla wanted to kill Karl, this didn't seem like the time to do it.

"So that day, Karl and I drove to the clinic separately. He left before me because he needed to check on a patient who's in the hospital. I left here about a quarter of eight, and those truffles were not in this house. I know because I've been doing these mindfulness exercises. You know, focusing on stillness and my breathing for a few minutes each day, and since the house was empty, I did them in the living room after Karl left. I would have noticed a plate of chocolates."

Alice folded her hands on the table, her gaze on Gail.

Gail continued. "Karl left the office about three thirty. I stayed finishing up some paperwork, and then I came home and..." She made a fluttery motion with her hands. "Well, you know the rest."

I did. And nothing she'd told us really helped. We might be able to prove that she'd been at the office all day, but she easily could have set out those truffles after Karl left for the hospital.

I rested an elbow on the table and propped my chin on

my hand. "Alice mentioned a key missing at the office. Is there anyone who works there you think might have killed Karl?" Hopefully, she'd mention Amber or Dr. Roth since they both had access.

Instead, Gail shook her head vigorously. "Absolutely not." She shifted slightly in her chair. "Oh, I know Karl could come across as a bit conceited, and sometimes be a little brusque, but we really are a family at Fairview Medical. There are issues, of course, but we all agree that patient care is the most important thing. And everyone at the clinic knew Karl always acted with the patient foremost in his mind."

Hmmm. Having met both Karl and Gail, I could picture office conversations ending the second Gail came in the room, with all her colleagues sparing her their true opinions of her husband.

"Are you sure?" Alice dipped her chin and looked across the table at Gail. "My Doug is a sweetheart, but sometimes his employees don't think so."

"I'm sure. Everyone at work liked and respected Karl." Gail sat up taller. "But I do know who the police should really be talking to."

"Who?" Alice and I said in unison.

"Gary Boyd, the contractor who was working on our basement. He knew the keycode, and he and Karl had a major argument a few days ago. Karl was so disappointed with Gary's work that he refused to pay the full amount, and he'd been telling his friends about the shoddy workmanship. Gary was furious."

I leaned forward. "Did you tell Detective Harper?"

"I did, but he didn't seem to take me seriously. Said he knew Gary and that he had a hot temper but that he never did anything, just got loud."

"Instead, the detective thinks you killed Karl," Alice said. "Ridiculous."

"We'll look into Gary and see what we can find out," I said.

Gail rested a hand on my arm. "Thank you, Libby. Thank you both so much."

A few minutes later she walked us to the door, and I headed back to the museum.

I didn't like the bit about Gail destroying evidence, but I had to admit Gary Boyd seemed like someone we should check out. He had both opportunity and motive for killing Karl.

Chapter Eight

FRIDAY NIGHT, I saw Cleo briefly before she left to spend the weekend in St. Louis, where she was attending a wedding. I told her what Alice and I had learned and found out that Cleo knew Gary. We made plans to talk to him on Monday.

After she left, I spent Friday evening hanging out with Bella. I administered her eardrops, which really seemed to be helping. Then I watched my favorite TV show, *Antiques Roadshow,* while looking forward to my date the next day with Sam. We planned to do some historical detective work, trying to figure out why Ivy had been painted out of the family portrait.

The next afternoon, I drove over to Sam's with Bella, who he'd made a special point of inviting. Sam had had a golden retriever growing up, and he adored Bella.

The views as I drove out Red Barn Road were breathtaking. The Ozark hills were awash with color, and the sun glinted off the water as we crossed Cedar Creek.

As I turned into Sam's driveway, I gazed ahead at Ashlington, gleaming in the sun. The pale peach Queen Anne-style house had been constructed in 1872 and featured a rounded front porch, a balcony above, and a turret. When I'd moved to Dogwood Springs and seen Ashlington for the first time in many years, I'd gotten a bittersweet ache in my chest. I missed my grandparents and the fun times I'd had visiting them at Ashlington as a child. Now, though, I knew my grandparents would be pleased with how well Sam was taking care of the place. The sight of the house being lived in and loved made me happy.

Or maybe it was just Sam that made me happy.

I parked and let Bella out. She raised her nose to the air and bounded across the yard after a rabbit.

Even though I was a couple of minutes early, and I hadn't even knocked, Sam stepped outside and waved. Had he been watching for me? I hoped so. Just the sight of him in jeans and a St. Louis Cardinals T-shirt made my heart beat faster.

Bella raced up to the porch and circled him until he petted her.

I walked closer and finally drew my eyes away from Sam long enough to notice the changes to the porch. Dozens of white and pinkish-bronze mums and teal, white, and pink-ish-peach pumpkins—all uncarved—were arranged in a display that looked gorgeous with the color of the house. "Wow, you've really decorated."

"It wasn't me." Sam came down the porch stairs to meet me. "When my interior designer learned Ashlington was going to be on the homes tour, she said I needed more accessories. What do you think?"

"If the inside is like this, I'm sure I'll love it, and the people on the tour will as well."

"I'm glad you like it." He took my hand and squeezed it.

Tingles ran through me, and I gazed up at him. "Today is going to be so much fun." A day with Sam, doing historical research, was about as perfect a day as I could imagine.

He gestured to the door. "C'mon in."

Inside, the decorator's work was evident. A new end table here, a lamp there, and several new pieces of artwork. I patted Bella and reminded her to stay calm. I certainly didn't want her to accidentally knock some expensive statue off a table with her tail.

"The place looks great," I said as I followed Sam into his study. "But I sure am glad your decorator isn't Monica Boyd."

"Me too." Sam brought his laptop over to a pair of chairs on the side of his office. "I have no interest in having a potential murderer in my house."

The two of us sat, and I couldn't help but be impressed with the buttery leather upholstery on the chairs. Sometimes, I was barely aware of how well-off Sam was. Other times, like when I noticed that the chair I was sitting in probably cost more than all the furniture in my apartment combined, his wealth was hard to ignore.

Bella, though, was unconcerned with finances. She

sniffed Sam's desk and the piles of paper on the floor around it, then flopped down on the carpet near us.

Sam's forehead furrowed. "You're being careful with the investigation, aren't you?"

"I haven't done much investigating yet, but when I do, I'll be careful."

He let out a heavy breath. "Good. I wouldn't want anything to happen to you." His voice held a note of real concern, and he looked at me for a long moment.

My heart melted a little, and I leaned toward him. "I won't do anything stupid. I promise."

His shoulders relaxed.

"Hey, I do have a question for you related to the murder. Alice and I sort of ruled out the housekeeper as a suspect because she posted a photo online of herself at her daughter's house in Texas, holding her new grandson." I hesitated. "This is crazy, but could that be faked? It didn't have a location tag or anything."

"How do you know the photo was taken in Texas?"

I explained about the Dallas Cowboys pennant on the wall behind them.

Sam gave me a look all too similar to one I'd gotten from Detective Harper. The one that said I was naïve. "People can live outside of Texas and be Cowboys fans," he said gently. "And did you ever hear of Photoshop?"

"Oh. Yeah." How stupid could I be? "So I guess the housekeeper is back on the list, which makes six suspects who might have killed Karl Wellston, if we don't include Gail."

Sam angled his head to one side. "You know, I've been in the Wellstons' home."

"You have?" He didn't seem like the type of person who would have enjoyed hanging out with Karl and his ego.

"Before they bought it. It was one of the houses the real estate agent showed me when I moved to town two years ago. If I remember right, at the time it belonged to a local woman named Cheryl Nichols."

"Really? I had no idea." So Cheryl, the landscaper, had owned that big Italianate home before the Wellstons. Would I ever get used to all the connections in a small town?

"I'm pretty sure that was her name. Of course once I saw Ashlington, I wasn't interested in that house in town anymore."

"Ashlington is pretty special." I gestured to his laptop. "Shall we check out the 1910 census? I've been really curious to learn if Ivy was still in town then."

"You bet." Sam turned on the laptop and navigated to a genealogy site with the records from the 1910 census.

Earlier, Sam had found Ivy listed in the 1900 census, but he'd waited until we could search together to look further. In 1900, Ivy had been thirteen and living with her parents. By 1910 she would have been twenty-three. Perhaps she had married someone her parents disapproved of, and that was why she'd been painted out of the portrait.

The genealogy site was fairly intuitive, but even so, Sam navigated it like a pro. I guess that came with being a tech genius. Easily enough, we found Ivy's parents, Horace and

Blanche, as well as her younger sister, Florence, listed as living in Dogwood Springs in 1910.

But there was no Ivy.

"Try the marriage records," I said. "If she got married, the census back then wouldn't include her maiden name. Just one of the reasons women can be a lot harder to trace than men."

Sam searched and searched but found no record of Ivy Whitfield getting married in Missouri or any other state, for that matter. He turned to me and twisted his mouth to one side. "Any other ideas?"

I thought for a moment. "Well, it wouldn't explain why she was painted out of the portrait, but she might have died."

"Should we look in the cemetery?" Sam's face brightened. "A field trip?"

I glanced out the window. "We might find the answers online, and of course an old gravestone might not be legible, but it really is a pretty day out."

Sam stood. "Let's go. Car, Bella?"

In an instant, she was at the front door, with Sam and me right behind her.

It was time to hunt for more clues.

I offered to drive, but Sam assured me that he had a blanket in his trunk that would protect his seats from Bella's toenails. So we took his blue Tesla with Bella riding in the back, poking her head up between the seats as if she, too, was eager to learn what had happened to Ivy.

The Dogwood Springs Cemetery was only a few blocks from my apartment. Sam drove through the gated cemetery entrance, down the narrow, paved path between the plots, and parked in the lot of a maintenance shed.

I fastened on Bella's leash and let her out.

The cemetery was well kept, with fresh-looking silk or plastic arrangements on many gravesites, as if family members visited often. Today, though, except for a blue jay that scolded us from a huge, gnarled red cedar, it appeared to be empty.

Of course, as a historian, I knew the history of the cemetery. Established in the 1850s, it had originally been a family cemetery on the highest hill of a local farm. During the Civil War, the cemetery had been used by the Union Army, and there were several civil war gravestones scattered about —each of them white, about eighteen inches tall, with a rounded top and a shield outlining the inscription.

There were other interesting old gravestones as well, like one with a tall white obelisk that looked almost like a small Washington Monument. There were some that were heartbreaking, like a gravestone for a brother and sister who died within a month of each other at ages eight and nine. And, of course, there were gravestones for members of my own family, including my grandparents and my great-great grandmother Elsie Dorsett, who was a bit of a local hero.

Back in the 1920s and '30s, Elsie had been mayor of the town and had been a real powerhouse. She changed the name to match the nearby Dogwood Springs. She convinced a railroad baron to donate funds to establish a teachers' college, now Grove University. And she worked to attract other businesses that would provide good-paying jobs, without "making things ugly," as she'd called it. Today, she'd be seen as an urban planner working to avoid pollution and protect the environment.

As her final beautification step, she'd made sure that every home was provided a young maple tree that would turn vivid red every fall and a small dogwood sapling.

In time, all those dogwoods in the spring and maples in the fall made the town the tourist favorite it was today. I rested a hand on Elsie's marker and thanked her for making the town so lovely.

Then Sam and I spread out, wandering around the older markers. I was bent over, struggling to read an inscription that had been mostly worn away when Sam let out a whoop.

"Libby! I've found a Whitfield," he cried.

Bella and I hurried over.

He showed me a marker for a John Whitfield, who died in 1950.

"I bet we're close, then." I scanned the area, searching for the oldest-looking markers in the family plot, which was delineated with a low concrete wall.

"Look," I said, pointing to a tall, narrow marker. "It's Florence, Ivy's younger sister. She never married and died in 1925. So she would have been…" Let's see, she was nine in 1900, so…

"Thirty-four," Sam said. "And here are her parents. Blanche and Horace ... and Mary?"

I read the birth and death dates on the intricately carved stones and studied the position of the graves, one woman on either side of Horace. "I bet Mary was Horace's first wife and probably Ivy's mother, given when Mary died."

"So Blanche was a stepmom," Sam said. "I wonder how she and Ivy got along?"

"Good question." I spotted a low stone marker nearby and knelt beside it.

Bella nosed her way in and blocked my view.

I gently elbowed Bella out of the way and pulled away some dead grass that hid the inscription, then drew in a sharp breath. "Sam." I pointed. "It's her."

The stone was not nearly as elaborate as her parents' or her sister's. It identified her as Ivy Anne Whitfield, born in 1887, died in 1905.

"Dead at only eighteen." Sam knelt beside me and rubbed moss off the inscription. "You'd think if she did something disgraceful enough to be painted out of the portrait, she might not be buried with her family."

I ran a hand across the cold, stone marker. "Maybe she died some tragic death, and the family was so grief stricken they couldn't look at her portrait?"

Sam wrinkled his nose. "I'd think the opposite, that they'd want to remember her."

"I know. I can't imagine why they painted her out. And, even in the early 1900s, if someone lived past childhood, eighteen is young to die, unless a woman died in childbirth."

Sam looked over at me. "Maybe she died giving birth to an illegitimate child."

"Maybe... We should try to find her obituary in the newspaper."

"Good idea," Sam said. "But we've done a lot for one day, finding out when Ivy died, and that she never married. How about we call it a day, pick up a pizza, and eat it at my house?"

I wasn't even hungry until he said the word pizza, but suddenly, my stomach growled. I laughed. "That sounds wonderful."

Sam grinned. "We could stop at your house to get Bella's dinner, and for dessert I've got some Minnesota's Pride ice cream in my freezer."

"Why am I not surprised?"

"Hey, you've got a thing for shortbread. You have to allow me my ice cream addiction," he said. "Besides, I bought a flavor I thought you'd like, Sugar Cookie Swirl."

Sugar Cookie Swirl sounded delicious. So did an evening with Sam.

Chapter Nine

THE NEXT DAY, while I did my laundry, I texted Cleo, Alice, and Zeke to tell them what Sam said about Marla and her photo with the new baby.

Zeke offered to go back through Marla's social media accounts and her daughter's accounts to look for clues, and said he'd blow up the image of her with the grandbaby and search for signs it had been digitally altered.

And Cleo and I confirmed our plans to talk to Gary on Monday.

Once I'd done all I could, I curled up on my couch and worked on a crossword.

On Monday, after I ate lunch early at my desk while answering emails, I met Cleo in the parking lot behind the museum.

I climbed into her old, red Jeep and moved a bag from the craft store out of the space at my feet and into the back seat. "More craft supplies?"

"Sorry. I should have moved that. I thought a new project might perk me up."

I glanced over at her. Despite Cleo's perfect hair and cute scarlet sweater, there was a droop in her posture. "You okay?"

"Yeah, just tired from the wedding. You know how it is when you spend time with people you haven't seen in years. You stay up way too late talking." She chuckled. "Rather than going to the craft store, it probably would have been cheaper to buy a bigger Diet Dr. Pepper."

I pointed to the enormous cup in the console. "I don't think a bigger one would fit."

"That's why cars come with two cupholders," she said. "For backup." She focused on the road and turned at a light.

I stared at her a moment longer. Maybe she was simply tired. But I was going to keep an eye on her. For now, though, we needed to talk to Gary. "So Gary's one of your clients?"

"Both Gary and Monica. I did her hair first, and I think she recommended me to him."

"Tell me about them." I settled back into my seat.

"Well, they're both in their early forties. Gary's got a good reputation as a builder. And he's local. Graduated from Dogwood Springs High." Cleo turned onto a county highway and picked up speed. "Monica's from Chicago. They met when Gary was there on vacation. I'm not sure she knew how small Dogwood Springs was when she agreed to move here. She's a really talented designer and does a lot of jobs out of town."

"Good to know."

Cleo drove another mile and turned into a long driveway that led to a tan, two-story modern home with a smaller house on one side of the lot. According to Cleo, that smaller house was the shared office space for Gary and Monica.

Cleo parked by the office, next to a row of rust-colored mums in black pots.

Inside, the office was tastefully decorated in shades of beige and brown, with forest green accents.

Near the front door, a young man sat at a desk. His blond hair was cut very short on the sides and longer on top, and his blue eyes lit when he saw Cleo. "My favorite hair stylist! How great to see you!"

"Hey, Freddie!" Cleo introduced us and told me that Freddie was Gary and Monica's administrative assistant.

"Brains behind the whole operation," Freddie said in a joking tone as he tapped his chest.

An attractive redheaded woman in her forties walked through the outer office, phone held to her ear. She covered the microphone for a moment and spoke to us. "He acts like it's a joke. It's not. Gary and I both might go out of business without him."

Freddie glanced down, and his cheeks grew pink.

The redheaded woman waved at Cleo and me, then headed down the hall. "No, I'm not kidding," she said into the phone. "I know things are difficult between us because of Karl, but you asked for my professional opinion. If you don't believe me, ask your real estate agent.

The pool is hideous. If you're not replacing it, it needs to come out."

"Monica." Cleo tipped her head toward the woman's back.

"Gary's expecting you." Freddie gestured to the first door down the hall, which was half open. "Just go on in."

Cleo led the way into a large, extremely tidy office that had been decorated in the same beige, brown, and forest green.

"Cleo, come on in." Gary stood and waved us toward two chairs across from his nearly empty desk. He was of medium build and had short brown hair, a couple of days' worth of stubble, and a face lined by the sun. "And you must be Libby," he said, giving me a friendly grin.

"I am. Thank you for meeting me. I—"

"She brought me along as a character reference," Cleo interrupted, just as we'd planned. "Libby has an odd question for you."

"So you said on the phone." He sat back in his chair and spread his hands wide, palms up, in front of him. "Let's hear it."

In the outer office, the phone rang. I heard Freddie answer it and tap rapidly on his keyboard.

I shook my head, pushing past the distraction. "Well, I'm the director of the local history museum, and you may have heard that we're planning a tour of local historic homes."

"I have indeed. Monica and I already have tickets." His eyes gleamed like he was looking forward to the event. "One of my workers, Tony Norton, and his wife, Kiara, own the Craftsman that you're showing. Plus the tour is what got the Wellstons interested in finally fixing their basement."

"It's the Wellstons I wanted to talk to you about." I paused. "This is awkward, but after what happened to Dr. Wellston, I don't know if Gail will want to continue to participate in the tour, and I feel I should wait a few days before I ask. It seems rude to bring it up when she's dealing with bigger things. If she doesn't want to participate, I'd love to add a different house to the tour, and I feel like I need to start trying to identify what house that might be."

"That makes sense," he said.

Cleo leaned in. "I thought maybe, since you do lots of renovations on old houses, you might know someone who owns a historic home and would be willing to be added to the tour at the last minute."

"There's no money involved, at least not for the home-owner," I said quickly. "It's a fundraiser for the museum. All the homeowner gets out of it is a chance to help the community and show off their home."

"Let me think." Gary stared off to one side. "I do think you already had some of the best historic homes in the area, but if you need to add one at the last minute…" Suddenly, he called out loudly, "Freddie, when do the McEwens get back in town?"

"Not until December 1," came the reply.

"That's what I was afraid of," Gary said. "I'll keep thinking, but I'm coming up dry."

"Thank you." I pulled a business card from my purse

and slid it across the desk. "If you think of someone, don't say anything to them, just give me a call, if you would. Maybe by then we'll have heard that Gail wants to go ahead with the tour, and I won't need an additional house."

"Will do."

I sat my purse back on the floor and gave my best dramatic sigh. "This would all be so much easier if Karl hadn't been killed. He seemed like such a nice man."

An odd expression passed over Gary's face.

Cleo leaned in. "I saw that look, Gary. Do you know a reason someone might have killed him?"

He cleared his throat. "Well, no offense, Libby, and I hate to speak ill of the dead ... but Karl was a jerk."

Cleo nodded, as if she wholeheartedly agreed. "What did he do to you?"

"My crew worked on his basement for three weeks, sealing a leak and finishing off the space, and he refused to pay and badmouthed me all over town. Said the work wasn't up to his standards." Gary sniffed. "As if the guy knew thing one about construction."

"Seriously?" I tried to appear as sympathetic as possible. "That's terrible."

"Yeah, I was pretty steamed and may have lost my temper with him. After Karl was murdered, Monica told me I should have kept my mouth shut, that the police might think I killed Karl."

"Gosh," I said. "I hope you have a good alibi that you can give them."

Gary waved a hand, as if brushing my concern aside. "I

was at a house on the other side of town all that day. I'm sure my crew would vouch for me. Besides, I would have gotten my money eventually. I'd probably have to get my lawyer to sue for the money and the court costs, but I'd get paid."

"What about your reputation as a builder?" Cleo said. "I'd be in a real mess if people started saying I gave bad haircuts."

Gary laughed. "Ah, Cleo, you don't have to worry. No one would believe that. And no one believed what Karl said about me. He had a reputation for pulling this kind of thing. I should have listened to the people who told me not to take the job."

"Well, thank goodness." I picked up my purse and set it on my lap, ready to leave. I wasn't sure I believed everything he said, but he had an alibi. "It sounds like you have nothing to worry about." I glanced over at Cleo to see if she was ready to leave.

"No worries for me." Gary leaned toward us. "But I do wonder…"

"You think you might know who killed Karl?" Cleo's voice rang with excitement.

Gary rubbed a hand over his mouth and looked away.

"Really, if you think you know someone who might have wanted him dead, you should say something." I tried to sound convincing.

"I guess you're right." He ran his thumb and pinky finger into his hairline, right at the two points where the hair was receding. Or being worn away, if this was what he did when he was stressed. "I just feel conflicted. Part of me thinks Karl deserves justice and part of me doesn't want to cause trouble for her."

"Who are you talking about?" Cleo asked softly.

"Cheryl Nichols."

"The landscaper?" Cleo said.

"Yep. Karl's the reason that her older sister, Denise, died. He was a good doctor, overall, I think, but Cheryl was furious when Denise died. Blamed Karl completely. And she and Denise and their younger sister, Rhonda, who I went to school with, were all really tight. I mean, Cheryl is nice, but I can understand why she might have killed Karl."

"Have you told the police?" I asked.

"No." Gary cleared his throat. "I should, I know. It's just that in spite of my suspicions, I like Cheryl. When Rhonda's husband died four years ago, Cheryl was right there with her, really helping her get through it. And it's been a while since Denise died. If that was the motive, it seems like Cheryl would have killed Karl earlier."

"That's a tough spot," Cleo said. "But if Cheryl's innocent, I don't see how it could hurt to mention what you know to the police. If she's not..." She tipped her hands palms up.

"You're probably right." He blew out a breath. "Well, I'll consider it. And I'll think about who might be good for the historic homes tour."

Cleo and I stood, and I thanked him.

We said goodbye to Gary, then to Freddie, and climbed into Cleo's Jeep.

Cleo put her key in the ignition and turned to me. "Well, well, well. We need to find out more about Cheryl."

"I agree." I wedged my big purse beside my feet and fastened my seatbelt. "Revenge can be a powerful motive for murder."

Chapter Ten

BACK AT THE MUSEUM, I found Alice talking with a man about volunteering, explaining how volunteers covered most of the shifts in the gift shop. I asked her to stop by my office when she was free. When she did, I told her what Gary said about Cheryl.

"Cheryl Nichols a murderer?" Alice's forehead crinkled. "I don't know her really well, but I find that hard to believe, no matter how much she loved her older sister."

"If Gail didn't kill Karl, somebody else had to. And Sam told me that Cheryl owned that Italianate home before the Wellstons. Maybe she kept a key."

Alice tipped her head to one side. "I guess she might have. But we already knew she had access to the house. She could have taken the key from Karl's office."

"True. The bond between sisters can be so strong, though. I think we need to look at her more closely."

"Well, if you want to speak with Cheryl," Alice said, "today's the perfect day."

"Why?"

"Tonight's the annual bulb sale that the hospital guild puts on. I'm headed there as soon as we close up here. Cheryl's the group treasurer, and she'll be there at least until seven, when the sale ends."

"Oh." Still a relative newcomer to town, I didn't even know there was an annual bulb sale. "What does the guild do with the money?"

"It's for pediatric patients. Every child, even one who only visits the ER, gets a little stuffed animal and, sometimes, when the nurses see a greater need, they send the child home with a few extras, like new pajamas."

Aww. There were a few exceptions, of course, like whoever had killed Karl Wellston, but in general, the people of Dogwood Springs were incredibly nice. And it was just like Alice to be involved. Not only did she volunteer at the hospital, but she loved plants almost as much as Cleo loved crafts.

Now that I knew Cheryl was volunteering at the bulb sale, it was harder to see her as a suspect. I didn't picture a murderer working to raise money to help children. But the event was the perfect opportunity to talk to her.

Alice suggested I come after six, as most people would stop by on their way home from work and be gone by then. I texted Cleo, and she agreed to go with me.

That evening, after I'd let Bella out, I did her eardrops

and fed her. Then I quickly ate a frozen dinner, and Cleo and I headed for the Dogwood Springs Hospital.

The hospital was on Hartley Road, a major east-west artery one block north of First Street. From what people had told me, the hospital sent patients to larger medical facilities for serious medical issues. But if a child got dehydrated from the flu, if a woman needed a mammogram, or if anything required a trip to the emergency room, the care was supposed to be quite good.

I pulled in and parked in front of the white, three-story building. On one side of the large parking lot, a long row of tables had been set up. We walked closer, and I could read the signs attached to the front of the tables that identified them as Narcissus, Tulip, Hyacinth, Crocus, Snowdrops, and Iris. Someone sat behind each table, ready to help customers. Even now, when it was close to six-thirty, shoppers wandered from table to table, purchasing bulbs and rhizomes.

"There's Alice," I said. "At the tulip table."

Cleo and I waved to Alice, who was bagging bulbs.

Cleo elbowed me. "Cheryl's the woman behind the crocus table."

At the moment, none of the shoppers were interested in crocus bulbs. Cheryl sat in a chair behind the table, writing on a legal pad.

She was slender, about fifty years old, and wore a brown jacket and jeans. She had shoulder-length blond hair with long bangs, a style that looked like an attempt to grow out a much shorter cut.

"Does her hair bug you?" I whispered to Cleo.

"You know it," she replied quietly. "It's almost as bad as yours was before you finally let me work on it."

I rolled my eyes at her and walked to the crocus table. Large color photos taped to the top of the table showed the types available—white, yellow, pale purple, deep purple, and a purple-striped one.

A small bowl of candy-apple saltwater taffy, a local favorite made by Mimi's Candies, sat at the edge of the table beside the photos as if it was a treat for shoppers.

On the other side of the table, Cheryl had piled several of the distinctive red-and-white checked wrappers of the taffy, shredded into small squares. Apparently, when business was slow, Cheryl had been snacking.

"Hi." I smiled at Cheryl and took a piece of taffy. I unwrapped it and tucked it in the side of my mouth, determined to slowly let it melt so I could enjoy the sweet, spicy flavor as long as possible.

I pointed to the photo of the purple-striped blossoms. "I live in an apartment. Could I grow a few of these in a pot inside?"

"You certainly could. That variety is a giant spring crocus with blossoms about"—she held her hands a few inches apart—"this big. They will be lovely in a pot."

Cheryl looked over at Cleo, and her eyes narrowed. "Cleo Anderson?"

Cleo nodded.

"I thought I recognized you," Cheryl said. "I know your parents."

Cleo and I introduced ourselves, and I explained that I was the director of the local history museum.

Cheryl's eyes lit. "Oh, yes, you're putting on the homes show. Karl Wellston mentioned it to me."

Talk about lucky. She'd given me the perfect opening.

"Such a horrible thing," I said. "I heard that someone poisoned the poor man. Did you know him well?"

"Fairly." She told me the price for the bulbs and took my money. "I take care of the plants at Fairview Medical. I was even there the morning he was killed. I'd done most of the job the day before but had to stop back to take care of a plant that I forgot. They moved it and..." She made an ah-well gesture with her hands, then packed my bulbs in a paper sack and labeled it with the variety. "Anyway, I was at the clinic that day before I drove over to Westfield to have lunch and go to the Westfield Nursery."

Cleo and I exchanged glances.

"We've been to that nursery," Cleo said. "It's a great place."

"One of my favorites," Cheryl said. "Fabulous plants."

Cleo tipped her head to one side. "Do you also know Gail?"

"I do." Cheryl handed me the sack with my bulbs. "I was on the phone with her yesterday. She wanted my advice about landscaping. She's planning to sell the house and thinking of taking out the pool before she puts it on the market, which would mean the whole backyard would need to be redone." Cheryl bit her lips together and shook her head. "Such a foolish idea. That pool is lovely. Only put in four years ago. Probably good for another forty years."

"I guess she has lots of decisions to make if she's thinking of selling. I can't imagine why someone would want to kill Dr. Wellston, though." I pursed my lips, trying to appear as if I was thinking. "Unless he wasn't a very good doctor."

Cheryl quickly looked over at me. "It's odd that you'd say that. There was a time, maybe five years ago, when I thought his negligence led to my older sister's death."

"Oh, my," Cleo said. She leaned in with the perfect expression of sympathy on her face. "Do you really think so?"

I sucked on my taffy and watched the interchange. Sometimes this sleuthing business was easy, especially when Cleo's hometown connections made people open up and a suspect was this forthcoming.

"It was foolish on my part." Cheryl sighed. "I think I was simply looking for someone to blame after she died from cancer. Later, I realized that Denise should have gone to the doctor as soon as she thought something was wrong, instead of living in denial. Dr. Wellston did everything he could, sending her to a top-notch specialist in St. Louis and trying to keep her comfortable at the end."

"I'm so sorry," I said. "It must have been awful to lose your sister."

"It was. There were three of us—Denise, the oldest. Rhonda, the baby. And me in the middle. Our parents died shortly after Rhonda graduated high school, and I think that made us especially close."

"Rhonda teaches at the high school, doesn't she?" Cleo said.

"She does. Happily married now with stepdaughters who adore her." Cheryl gestured to the photos of the crocuses. "Seeing her stepdaughters growing up, seeing spring bulbs come up out of the snow … it helps remind me that life goes on. Good things can come after tragedy."

"I couldn't agree more," I said. Cheryl seemed at peace with the past, not likely to have killed Karl Wellston over her sister's death. "But poor Gail. I can't help but wonder why someone would have killed Karl, and I can't believe it was her."

Cheryl's eyes narrowed. "That's it. I remember you from the paper. You helped solve those two murders in the summer. Are you investigating Karl's death?"

"Not officially or anything. Just asking a few questions. I like things to make sense, and his death doesn't."

She looked off to one side, then spoke more softly. "I can understand your doubts about Gail, but... You never know about people's marriages, do you?" She rubbed her earlobe, as if her earring was bothering her. "But I do think I have another idea why Karl may have been killed."

"You do?" Cleo and I spoke in unison and edged closer.

"When I was at the clinic the morning of the day he was killed, I overheard him firing Amber, one of the nurses."

A zing of excitement shot through me. Cleo's friend had

said Amber went down the hall to Karl's office twice, and the first time she'd been upset. Could that have been because she'd been fired, and later she went back to steal the key to his house?

Cleo nodded at Cheryl. "If Amber was mad enough about being fired, that does sound like a possible motive."

"He was pretty mean about it," Cheryl said. "She left his office crying."

"Interesting." I rolled the edge of the paper sack with my bulbs between my fingers. "Have you told the police?"

"I did."

"Good. Hopefully, they'll ask Amber some questions. It seems like she might be a suspect."

Cleo and I wandered around the bulb sale a bit longer. I bought some paperwhite narcissus bulbs to force with my crocus, and we stopped by to talk to Alice.

But we kept the conversation light, not mentioning what Cheryl had said. The tables were too close together, and I didn't want Cheryl to know that our casual conversation about Karl had been planned.

She seemed like a nice woman. No need for her to know that I'd suspected her of murder.

Especially if Amber might have been the killer.

Chapter Eleven

THE NEXT DAY was Halloween and, luckily for the trick-or-treaters, the weather promised to be lovely. The high was expected to be about seventy-five, and temperatures all evening would be in the sixties.

Since I knew we'd be busy in the evening, I got up a half hour early so I could take Bella for an extra-long walk before work.

We headed down Elm Street, passed Thirteenth Street where we normally turned around, and continued all the way to Eighteenth Street before we turned back. As we returned, we met a group of children waiting for the school bus at Ninth and Elm Streets, all in costume, and all bubbling with excitement. Bella went up to every child, making sure they each had a chance to pet her. I wished them a happy Halloween and told them all to be sure to trick-or-treat at our house, the one between Fourth and Fifth Streets with the ghost.

Eventually, Bella and I got back to our apartment, and I pondered how to talk to Amber. Neither Cleo, nor Alice, nor Zeke knew her. I'd even texted Imani last night, but she didn't know Amber either.

What I needed was a reason to knock on the door of a total stranger and ask her if she'd committed murder.

I thought and thought but couldn't come up with a way to manage that.

An hour later, though, when I got to work, I found an answer.

Earlier, as part of our social media campaign about the homes tour, I'd posted that we were giving away four pairs of tickets to the event. Commenting on the post would enter a person to win.

When I checked the comments, I found that an Amber Riley had entered the contest. I checked her social media profile to make sure, and it was her.

If Amber happened to win, I could deliver her tickets in person, and, if I got her talking, maybe learn a thing or two.

But drawing her name on purpose wouldn't be fair to everyone else who entered.

Finally, I counted the number of entries, used a random number generator four times, and counted down from the first entry to find the post that matched each of the random numbers.

None of my four winners was Amber. After a brief ethical debate, where I decided that finding the killer was a greater good and that my lie wasn't hurting anyone, I went downstairs. I paid Imani for two tickets with my own money and declared Amber a "winner." I posted the five winners online, saying we'd given an additional pair of tickets as a surprise, and called Amber to tell her she'd won.

She answered on the second ring and sounded incredibly happy to learn she was a winner.

I offered to drop off her tickets and made arrangements to stop by that afternoon.

I had a bit of momentary panic when I remembered that I'd told Sam I'd be careful. Going to the apartment of a potential murderer alone didn't sound all that safe. I called Alice, and she agreed to go with me. Ideally, in a dangerous situation, I'd have asked Cleo, who had taken self-defense classes when she lived in New York. But it was a lot more believable for Alice, the president of the museum's board, to come along. She could take a photo of me presenting the tickets and we could post it on social media.

Midafternoon, I picked up Alice from the library, where she was volunteering, and we drove to Amber's apartment.

Unlike my apartment, a place with some historic character, Amber lived in a complex with at least ten buildings, eight units in each. They were new, nice, and—in my opinion—boring, although they probably had windows that were a lot more energy efficient than the ones in my apartment.

"There's building eight." Alice pointed. "Unit 801 should be in it."

I parked, and we easily found 801, a ground-floor unit. I knocked on the door.

Amber answered almost immediately, swinging the door

open wide and gesturing us in. She was in her forties, short, and stocky, and had dark brown hair that looked as if she'd chopped it off herself at chin-length. In honor of Halloween, she wore black jeans, an orange T-shirt, and black bat earrings.

"I'm so excited." Her dark eyes sparkled. "It's been a terrible week and then to win something, it gave me hope, you know, that things could get better."

Guilt twisted in my stomach, but I ignored it. So what if she hadn't technically won? The free tickets were bringing her a bit of happiness. If she wasn't the murderer, that was a good thing.

She led us into her living room, which she'd decorated in a western style with a Navajo rug, deer antlers over her gas fireplace, and cowhide pillows on her couch. A large dark green candle with three wicks sat on the mantel, and the air smelled faintly of pine. Narrow bookshelves flanked the fireplace. While Alice chatted with Amber, I scanned the shelves. The bookcase on one side held fiction, and the other was full of cookbooks and textbooks, including a large, thick book about medications. Exactly the type of book that might explain how many sleeping pills it took to kill a person.

Near the couch, a rustic coffee table held a large bowl of snack-size Almond Joy and Milky Way candy bars, ready for trick-or-treaters. Amber hurriedly scooped some empty wrappers off the coffee table and shoved them in her pocket.

Alice posed us near the fireplace, and I officially

presented the tickets. "Congratulations! I hope you really enjoy the tour."

"I will." Amber's words rang with enthusiasm, and she set the tickets on the coffee table, near the candy bowl. "I already called my best friend to invite her to go with me, and we're planning to make a weekend of it—the tour on Saturday and the museum on Sunday."

Exactly what we hoped people would do. I even had extra volunteers lined up to work that Sunday afternoon.

Not only did Amber seem nice, but she was also interested in history. But I needed to think of her as a suspect. I slid into the script Alice and I planned on the way over. "I'm not totally sure if there will be four houses or five on the tour."

"One of the homes we hoped to show was that of Dr. Karl Wellston," Alice said.

"I understand," Amber said. "And I've seen the Wellston home. I, uh, I'm a nurse, and I used to work at Fairview Medical. The Wellstons had us over for a Christmas drop-in last year. It's a beautiful home, but if Gail is grieving, it makes sense that she might not want to do the tour."

"Nursing is such a wonderful profession," Alice said. "Where do you work now, dear?"

Amber's face tensed. "Nowhere." She crumpled onto the couch and covered her face with her hands.

Alice and I quickly sat down on either side of her.

Alice patted her shoulder. "I'm so sorry. I didn't mean to upset you."

"I know. It's not you. I'm just a mess. I'm so afraid the

police are going to show up at the door, thinking I killed Dr. Wellston because he fired me the morning he died." She sniffed loudly. "He yelled at me so much that I got upset and dropped my phone. I had to go back later, sneak into his office when he was with a patient, and crawl around on the floor to find it."

Believable? Yes. But was it the truth? Maybe if I pushed a little, I could learn more. "Dr. Wellston wasn't killed at his office. From what I hear, he wasn't killed in the morning. The police would want to know what you were doing that afternoon."

Amber let out a moan. "Sitting right here, trying to drown my sorrows in wine. No one can give me an alibi." She sniffed again.

Alice pulled a tissue from her purse and handed it to her.

Amber blew her nose. "It's so unfair. I mean, once I get over the embarrassment of being fired, I know I can get another job. The clinic I worked for before Fairview will give me a good reference. It's not like I did something that affected patient care. I was just late for work too many times, and Dr. Wellston is—was—such a stickler about that."

"I'm sure you'll get a great new position," Alice said. "And most likely, the killer left physical evidence at the scene. DNA, you know? If you haven't been in the Wellstons' house since last Christmas, I wouldn't worry about it."

Amber sat up taller, and her words poured out. "Oh my

gosh, that makes perfect sense. Thank goodness. The police probably won't even want to talk to me." Her voice grew stronger, more resolute. "They can focus on the real killer."

Something about the way she emphasized the word *real* made me think she was referring to a specific person. I leaned closer. "You think Gail did it?"

"Gail?" Amber shook her head so vigorously that her black bat earrings bounced. "No way. I mean Dr. Roth."

I raised an eyebrow. "Edward Roth?" That had been one of the people who went down the hall, but I assumed it was because his office was near Karl's. "Why would he kill Dr. Wellston?"

"Because he was furious about how little he got paid. I mean, it wasn't little compared to what I made, but compared to Dr. Wellston, it was. And Dr. Roth saw like three times the patients Dr. Wellston did."

"Wouldn't the compensation plan have been explained to Dr. Roth before he joined the practice?" Alice asked.

"Apparently, Dr. Wellston had said one thing, and had a different thing in the paperwork. Dr. Roth didn't figure it out until after he'd moved to Dogwood Springs. And he didn't realize how few patients Dr. Wellston saw until he himself started. I mean, it will be a pain if I have to move to Jefferson City or St. Louis to get a job, but there are lots of nursing jobs. I think it's harder for a physician to find the right practice."

"Then I think, if the police do happen to show up at your door, you need to tell them all of this," I said. "Dr. Roth sounds like a very good suspect."

Amber nodded and stood, her cheeks growing pink. "I can't believe I told you all this. I'm sorry."

"Nothing to apologize for," Alice said gently. "You're going through a difficult time, and without meaning to, we brought up a touchy subject."

"I hope the homes tour can still be fun for you." I picked up my purse and took a step toward the door.

"It will be," Amber said. "I love seeing how people decorate their homes. I especially want to see the house where that rich guy lives, Ashlington. And maybe meet him. I've heard he's hot." Her eyes gleamed.

Really, that was why she wanted to go on the tour? I'd thought she was interested in history.

"Goodness, look at the time." Alice picked up her purse. "We'd better head on to our next appointment."

We said our goodbyes and headed out toward my car.

Once we were inside, Alice burst out laughing.

"What's so funny?" I turned on the engine and put the car in gear.

"Your face when Amber said Sam was hot." Alice grinned. "You've got it bad for that man, Libby Ballard. You've got it bad."

I rolled my eyes and pulled out into the street. We needed to focus on finding the killer, not my relationship with Sam.

We were making progress with the case, learning more and more.

Originally, I'd felt bad when Karl died because I didn't like the man. The further we dug, though, the more it seemed that almost no one liked him. And of the people who had access to his house to leave the poisoned chocolate truffles, an awful lot of them had a reason to hate him.

As soon as I got back to the museum, I sent a text to Cleo and Zeke telling them what Alice and I had learned.

It was time to investigate Dr. Roth.

Chapter Twelve

THAT EVENING, after I put the mystery item, still in its box, on Imani's desk, I left the museum right at five and hurried home. I let Bella out, did her eardrops, and fed her. Then I gobbled down some leftovers and had us both in our costumes by six o'clock, all ready for two hours of trick or treat.

Cleo met us on the porch and took in Bella's costume. "Oh, how cute!"

Bella wore a white furry vest that closed with Velcro over her chest, a hood with holes where her ears stuck out, and two tall white ears with pink satin lining and padded wire inside that made them stand up. The back of the vest hung down to cover her tail and instead showed a round, puffy white tail.

"You make an adorable bunny, Bella. The children are going to love you!" She turned to me. "And you are...?"

"I'm Bella." I wore a beige sweatshirt and sweatpants

and a cap that strapped under my neck that had two big, floppy dog ears. I'd added a dog collar around my neck and blackened my nose with face paint. "Just in case there's any barking, I can say it was me." I grinned. "But wow. Look at you."

Cleo was dressed as a pirate. She wore a black hat with gold trim, loose purple pants tucked into high-heeled black boots, and a flowing white blouse. Strapped to her waist was a purple sheath for a sword. She looked appropriate for trick-or-treat night, but her costume was far more stylish and flattering than mine, dressy enough for Halloween at a nightclub.

"You like?" She turned in a circle, then pulled out her plastic sword and struck a pose.

"You look great."

She swept her sword to one side, bowed deeply, and gestured to the two Adirondack chairs. She'd already moved them halfway to the sidewalk, so the trick-or-treaters would have a shorter distance to walk. "Go ahead and sit down. I'll be right back." She ran inside and returned with our big bowl of candy.

Once we were in position, we sat, listening to Haunting Harold, who Cleo had turned up to top volume, and congratulating ourselves on our choices of candy. We had some excellent snack-size chocolate choices, as well as Tootsie Pops, Smarties, and small bottles of bubbles for kids with food allergies.

At one minute past six, our first group of trick-or-treaters arrived. A witch, a vampire, and Dorothy from *The*

Wizard of Oz each took a piece of candy, said thank you, and petted Bella before running to the next house.

Up and down the street, other groups of kids went from house to house, most with a parent trailing behind. With the nice weather and the full moon that should be rising soon, I couldn't imagine a better Halloween.

Haunting Harold was a big hit. Even the youngest trick-or-treaters laughed at him, and several kids had their moms take their photo with him.

I ate a KitKat bar, enjoying the mix of crunch and chocolate, and settled in to enjoy the evening.

A few minutes later, Sam arrived. He parked in our driveway and pulled a folding chair from his trunk. "Mind if I join you? I don't get very many trick-or-treaters out in the country, and I brought candy." He held up two bags of little Snickers bars.

"We'd love to have you join us." I scooted my chair, making a spot for him in the middle, closer to the sidewalk.

Bella ran to greet him and, after he'd given her sufficient attention, walked over with him.

Sam poured one bag of candy into our bowl and stashed the other bag on the porch. Then he sat down, said hello to Cleo, and turned to me. "You know, I used to think Bella was the cutest golden retriever in town. I see she has competition." He shot me a look that made my heart race.

"Um, uh, where's your costume?" I finally managed to ask.

"I'm wearing it." He held out his hands as if displaying a

costume. "This is a very close facsimile of what a college professor looks like."

Cleo rolled her eyes. "Sam, that's lame."

He tipped his head in acknowledgement. "I know. I'm not much for dressing up, but I like to see the kids in their costumes." He grabbed a Snickers bar. "And I like the candy. So I decided at the last minute to stop by. I knew you would get lots of trick-or-treaters."

"I'm glad you came by." I rested a hand on his arm. "It makes it more fun."

A trio of boys raced up who all looked somewhere between eight and ten. I didn't recognize their costumes and didn't even know what they were once they told me. But Sam talked to each boy about his character while Cleo held out the candy bowl. The boys took some and ran toward the next house.

I turned to Sam. "Wow, they really lit up when you talked to them. What exactly were they?"

"They're characters from Planet Zorba."

Cleo and I exchanged confused glances.

"What's Planet Zorba?" she asked.

"It's a video game. Very popular with kids that age. Not much violence, so parents are usually okay with it."

"Oh." I'd never heard of it. "I—"

Sam's phone rang.

He pulled it out of his pocket. "Sorry, I need to take this." He stood and stepped back toward the house. From what Cleo and I could hear from his side of the conversation, something was wrong.

Another group of trick-or-treaters arrived.

By the time they were gone, Sam was refolding his chair. "Sorry, Libby, Cleo, but I've got to go. That was my department chair. An older member of the department, Roscoe Brown, had a massive heart attack this afternoon."

"Oh my." I stood.

"He's headed into surgery, and the doctors are quite hopeful, but he won't be teaching for a while. And I'm the only other person in the department who can teach his classes. I have to meet the department chair tonight to be ready to teach at eight tomorrow morning."

Cleo expressed her sympathy, and I walked with Sam to his car. "Keep me posted on Professor Brown."

"I will." Sam gave me a quick kiss and drove away.

I moved my chair back next to Cleo. For a while, we were subdued, but she reminded me that Sam said the doctors were quite hopeful. Between that and the cute kids that came by, our spirits lightened.

About an hour later, when trick or treat was almost over, a man about my age and a young girl about three or four came down the sidewalk toward our house. The girl pointed to Bella and tugged on the man's arm.

"Okay," he said, laughing.

As they drew closer, I realized why the little girl had been intrigued by Bella. The girl was wearing an almost identical bunny costume, only little-kid sized, not extra-large-dog sized.

The girl ignored the bowl of candy, petted Bella, and, after seeing how friendly Bella was, hugged her.

Bella rubbed her head against the little girl's head, making both of their bunny ears wobble.

"Good bunny." The girl petted Bella and giggled. "Such a good bunny."

Bella gazed up at her as if she made the whole costume nonsense worth it. When the little girl leaned down to kiss her, Bella licked her cheek.

The girl giggled even louder.

"Do you mind if I get a picture, Cleo?" The man pulled out his phone.

"No. That's fine." Cleo had an odd expression on her face, like she was trying on shoes a size too small.

"Bella would love to be in a photo," I said quickly. He seemed like a nice guy. Average height, average build, average brown hair, and hazel eyes. A run-of-the-mill dad-next-door. "That's her name," I said, gesturing to Bella. "And I'm Libby."

"Bryce Parker," the man said. "And this is my niece, Evie."

I held out the candy bowl.

Evie took a Tootsie Pop, dropped it in her plastic pumpkin bucket, and said thank you. Then she turned back to Bella.

Bryce chuckled. "Evie's more interested in people's pets than she is in candy, but I guess that runs in the family."

"Oh?" I looked up at him.

"He's a vet," Cleo said. "Same practice as your vet. Great seeing you again, Bryce." Her voice tightened. "Say hello to Darcy for me."

His face tensed. "I will. C'mon, Evie. We have other houses to visit."

Evie kissed Bella's forehead and skipped away with her uncle.

Bella laid her head on my knee and let out a sad little sigh.

I petted her and assured her that more children would be visiting.

As soon as Bryce and Evie were out of earshot, I turned to Cleo. "Who was that?"

Cleo's eyes clouded, and she sank deeper into her chair. "Remember how I told you when we first met that I moved to New York to study hair design and later I moved back?"

"I do."

"Bryce is the reason I came back. We were pretty serious in high school, but I was an idiot when I was seventeen. I decided he was boring, broke up with him, and started dating a guy named Jimmy Sykes."

I unwrapped another KitKat. This guy Bryce must have been a big deal in Cleo's life. Why had she never mentioned him?

"I eventually figured out that Jimmy was a jerk. And years later, after I'd dated a whole bunch of guys in New York, I finally figured out that I never should have broken up with Bryce."

"So you moved back, hoping to get together with him again?"

"Stupid, right? But I did. Four years ago." Cleo's mouth twisted to one side. "Normally doing things spontaneously works out great for me, but not this time. I'd heard he was dating Darcy Jackson, who was in the same class in school with us, but that they were about to break up. I thought I'd be there to pick up the pieces and apologize for dumping him all those years ago."

"Only they didn't break up?"

"No." Cleo—the woman who ate her candy in small bites to make it last—ripped open a snack-sized Baby Ruth and shoved the whole thing in her mouth. "They didn't break up," she mumbled around the candy. "They got engaged."

"Oh." Wow. "When did they get married?"

She chewed and swallowed. "They're still engaged."

"Four years later?"

"Uh-huh." She dug another Baby Ruth out of the candy bowl.

"That's a little odd. Like maybe Bryce really doesn't want to marry Darcy."

"That's what my mom says. But they're still together." Cleo ripped open the wrapper and bit the little Baby Ruth in half.

Now I understood why she had seemed down after attending a wedding. It reminded her of Bryce. And I felt rather bad that Sam had stopped by earlier, like I'd been rubbing my relationship in her face. Had I been so wrapped up in my divorce and meeting Sam that I'd ignored the fact that she was miserable?

No, she went out with guys from time to time, but she never seemed to date anyone more than two or three times.

I'd attributed it to her personality, but clearly it was something more. All these years later, Cleo was still in love with Bryce.

But waiting around for him wasn't working. Even if Bryce and Darcy hadn't gotten married, he was in a serious relationship. Cleo needed to move on.

And one thing still didn't make sense. "Why didn't you go back to New York after you learned he got engaged?"

She wiped some chocolate from her lips. "Well, after I was living back in Dogwood Springs again, I realized how much I'd missed it. I like being around my family and knowing everyone and the fact that five minutes is a long commute."

"That is nice," I admitted. "And personally, I'm very glad you moved back home. I'd never have known you if you hadn't." I reached over and squeezed her arm. "But I'm sorry you have to run into Bryce from time to time."

"I'm sure I'll get over him eventually." Cleo let out a heavy sigh. "One of these days, I'll find a guy who I'll like even more."

"I'm sure you will." Especially if I started keeping an eye out for someone to introduce her to. It might take a while, but maybe Sam would be able to suggest someone. Cleo was my best friend, and I wanted her to be happy.

Chapter Thirteen

THE NEXT MORNING, Sam texted. He only had a minute before he had to teach, but he wanted to let me know that Professor Brown had come through surgery and was doing well.

I thanked him. Then, while I ate some instant strawberry oatmeal and Bella crunched on her kibble, I looked up Edward Roth on the Fairview Medical Practice website.

Neither Cleo nor Alice knew him, which struck me as odd. Maybe he hadn't been in town that long.

Still, it made it harder to think of an easy way to talk to him.

Finally, I messaged Cleo and asked her to check with her friend who was a receptionist at Fairview Medical. If I knew what time Dr. Roth normally left the office, I could hang around outside the clinic and casually bump into him after work. Perhaps the straight-out approach, asking him to help me in order to help Gail, would work.

An hour later, Cleo texted back. Except for a rare exception, Dr. Roth left the building at about five thirty each day.

Excellent. I could drive to work after lunch, zip home to let Bella out right after five, and easily be at the clinic by five thirty.

Unfortunately, though, no one else was available to go with me.

Still, how dangerous could it be to talk to him in front of a doctors' office in broad daylight? "You'll go with me, right Bella?"

She gave a willing woof.

I quickly dressed, gave Bella extra attention, and headed to work.

Late in the morning, Alice called. She'd talked to Gail, who apologized for not thinking about the homes tour sooner. If we thought people would still want to see their home, she was fine with it. I thanked Alice, asked her to thank Gail, and shared the news with Imani and Rodney.

I had lunch at home with Bella, then drove back to the office and spent the whole afternoon working on a grant proposal.

By five I was more than ready to leave, and at five thirty, Bella and I were casually strolling along the sidewalk outside the two-story brick building that housed the Fairview Medical Practice, looking for the man I'd scoped out on the practice website. The building was located near the hospital, between a fast-food place and a driving range, which meant other foot traffic went by. It seemed perfectly safe.

Bella and I were on our second pass in front of the building when a tall, slender man walked out. Short, dark hair with a receding hairline, a narrow face, and a long chin, just like the photo on the website—Dr. Edward Roth.

Bella's ears perked up, and she led me toward him.

"Well, hello." He stopped and, when Bella rubbed her head against his leg, gave her a pat.

Really, I was so lucky to have Bella help me with investigating. In the past, she'd introduced me to people who helped me find clues, and now she was smoothing the way for me to meet a suspect I needed to question.

I stepped closer. "Dr. Roth?"

He turned his head toward me with a jerk. "Do I know you?" He spoke slowly, his tone guarded.

Uh-oh. This conversation might be tricky. "We've never met. I'm Libby Ballard, and this is Bella."

He looked at me, then at Bella.

Bella rubbed her head against his leg, and the muscles in his jaw eased. A second later he began petting her.

Good job, Bella!

I gave Dr. Roth my best smile. "I'm sorry to bother you, but I was hoping you might have a moment to talk with me. I'm trying to help Gail Wellston. She said you might have some idea why someone would have killed Karl."

His forehead furrowed, but his eyes looked interested, not defensive. "Are you a private detective?"

"No, I'm actually the director of the town history museum. I'm just helping out as a friend. The police suspect Gail, and she's desperate to give them someone else to consider. I thought perhaps you might have noticed something."

He rolled his eyes. "Seriously? The cops think Gail Wellston killed Karl? That's as ridiculous as the rumor people are whispering about in the office that I killed him."

Whoa. I'd thought this guy would be hard to question. *Thank you, Bella!* I tried to appear intrigued instead of gleeful. "Why would you kill Karl?"

"An argument about compensation." He sniffed. "But I was in the office seeing patients at the time those rumor mongers say Karl was killed. Plus, I already had an offer from a practice in Jefferson City. Why would I kill him when I'm planning to move somewhere better anyway?"

Better than Dogwood Springs? I opened my mouth to disagree, then closed it. For someone who'd had serious doubts about the town five months ago, I was all-too-ready to defend it now, and I needed to focus on the case.

"That doesn't make much sense as a motive." I looked him in the eye. "You're clearly a smart man. Did anything stand out to you that seemed odd?"

He shifted his weight from one foot to the other. "You'll be telling Gail?"

"Ye-es." I didn't understand what he was getting at.

He made an odd movement where he stretched his shoulders up while running his hands down his pant legs. Then he looked back at me. "I don't really want to be the reason Gail learns the truth, but I guess it's better than going to prison for a crime she didn't commit." He gestured to a bench in front of the clinic.

The two of us sat down, and Bella sat at his side.

He continued petting her, as if drawing comfort from her presence, and turned to me. "If I had to guess, I'd say the murder was related to Karl's affair."

"Affair?" I sat back against the bench. "I had no idea he was having an affair."

"Neither does Gail. The woman is too nice for her own good." He shook his head. "For about four months, Karl's been seeing the woman who's decorating his house, Monica Boyd. So my number one suspect would be her husband, Gary." He stood and gave Bella another pat. "I hope you can find someone the police will suspect instead of Gail. She doesn't deserve any of this. I've got to go." He walked toward a black sports car parked all alone at the far side of the lot to the side of the medical building, as if he didn't trust other drivers not to ding it.

I got to my feet and looked at Bella. "Wow." If Karl Wellston was having an affair, it put a whole different spin on things.

"Psst."

I looked around, and Bella tipped her head to one side, tags jingling.

Kiara Norton, co-owner of the Craftsman bungalow that would be on the homes tour, peeked out from behind a tall arborvitae bush. "Is Dr. Roth gone?"

I kept facing the parking lot but edged back toward the arborvitae. "Just a minute."

The sports car left the parking lot, turned a corner, and

disappeared from view. "Now he's gone," I said to the arborvitae.

Kiara stepped out from behind the evergreen. She was a short woman with an Afro cut very close on the sides, and she wore light green scrubs and a navy-blue sweater. "I didn't want him to know I was eavesdropping, but I have to tell you, everything he said is true. Karl was having an affair with Monica. I don't know if her husband, Gary, knew about it. But if he did, he's got quite a temper. My husband works for him, so I should know."

I nodded. Gary had mentioned that as well.

"Personally, I'd suspect Monica," Kiara said, leaning down to pat Bella. "Karl treated women like dirt, but unlike Gail, who's too nice to even notice, Monica has a backbone."

"Oh, so she might have gotten sick of the way he treated her and—"

"And decided the world would be better without Dr. Karl Wellston." Kiara pulled her cardigan closed and buttoned it. "I'd better get home, but I wanted you to know. I'm glad you're trying to find the real killer. I don't think it's Gail." She gave a quick wave and walked toward the parking lot.

"Thanks," I called after her. Then I tugged on Bella's leash, and the two of us headed toward my Camry. It was time to reheat some leftovers for dinner, have a cup of hot tea, and think about all the clues.

～

The next day was Thursday, normally a busy day for Cleo, but once I told her what I'd learned from Dr. Roth and Kiara, she said she'd try to get free so we could talk to Monica. We'd already talked to Gary once and only gotten part of the story. Maybe Monica would be more forthcoming.

"I'll call one of my regulars," Cleo said. "She's retired and has told me several times that if I ever need to juggle her appointment a little, she won't mind a bit. If I can get her to come in half an hour early, I can be free from eleven-thirty to twelve thirty. Would that work?"

"I can make it work," I said. That grant proposal wouldn't care a bit when I took my lunch hour. And Thursday's lunch, a leftover enchilada and some rice and beans, would taste just as good later in the day while I read emails at my desk.

By eleven forty, we were parked in front of the little tan office with the rust-colored mums out front. I switched off my engine. "How do we play this?"

"I think we confront her," Cleo said.

Direct confrontation was not really my style, but Cleo knew Monica. I didn't. I'd have to trust her.

Freddie greeted us and sent us right back to Monica's office, which was a clone of her husband's only far less tidy and filled with the strong smell of burned microwave popcorn.

"Great dress," Cleo said as she knocked on the open door.

It was. The dark green velvet was perfect with Monica's

red hair and fair coloring, and the fabric hugged her figure like it was made for her.

She dipped her head, murmured "thanks," and waved us in. "What brings you all by?"

Cleo and I sat down in the chairs across the desk from Monica.

Cleo leaned in. "Did you kill Karl because you were having an affair and he was a jerk to you?"

Monica's mouth dropped open, then she got up and shut the door. "Cleo, are you nuts? What if Gary was in the office?"

"His car's not here," Cleo said calmly.

"He's off at a job site, but sometimes he parks at the house," Monica said.

Cleo cringed. "I'm sorry. He doesn't know?"

Monica shrank down in her chair. "Actually, he does, but he'd be royally peeved to think that other people know. How did you find out?"

"People in Karl's office knew," I said. "And they're speculating that you killed him."

Monica's face fell. "Oh. My. Word. What a mess." She pressed both hands to her mouth, then let them fall to her lap. "And I have no alibi. Freddie was home sick the day of the murder. I brought my lunch and didn't leave the office all day, but there's no one who can verify that."

"I figured you'd rather know what's being said, so you can deal with it," Cleo said.

Monica sighed. "Yeah, I guess so. Karl and I had been involved. But he ended things about a week before he was killed." She shrugged. "I had been planning to stop seeing him anyway, but I let him think it was his idea, so ... well, so he'd feel guilty. Anytime he annoyed me, he charmed his way back into my heart with jewelry." She hesitated. "I, uh, I thought I might get some diamond earrings out of it." She gave an awkward laugh, as if maybe, once she said it out loud, she realized how manipulative that sounded.

I tried not to let my disapproval show. "Pretty much everyone in town knows that your husband had an argument with Karl not long before the murder. Was that really about the affair?"

"No, that was about the work Gary and his crew did in Karl's basement." Her eyes narrowed. "Gary's no killer. And as far as the affair is concerned, Gary doesn't blame Karl. He blames me." She sighed. "I wish I'd never gotten involved with Karl. I'm hoping Gary and I can work things out."

I wasn't sure I believed anything she was saying, but if she wasn't the murderer, she might have an idea who was.

"You must have spent a lot of time with Karl," I said. "Did he ever say anything that made you suspect someone might want to kill him?"

Monica leaned in, elbows on her desk. "If I was the cops, I'd suspect Gail. I wasn't Karl's first fling, and I wouldn't have been surprised if he had someone else waiting in the wings. He said something once that made me think Gail knew and was getting sick of it."

I looked over at Cleo. If Monica was telling the truth, we were right back to square one.

Cleo assured Monica that if anyone brought up her name in connection to the murder, she'd do her best to squelch it.

We said goodbye to Monica and then to Freddie and headed back downtown.

We needed to talk to Gail again.

Despite the fact that she was Alice's friend, despite how much people liked her, Gail could easily have left the poisoned chocolates for her husband. She had destroyed evidence. And she had a strong motive for murder.

Chapter Fourteen

FIRST THING FRIDAY MORNING, Imani walked into my office and set the box with the mystery item on my desk.

"I know Rodney's out for the day with that doctor's appointment, but I don't need this anymore. I know exactly what it is, and I bet you do too." Her eyes twinkled.

"I do indeed. You often see these in a smaller size, but really, he's going to have to try harder if he wants to stump us."

"I might stumble on some farming tool, but this was easy. But maybe not for Rodney. I can't ever see him using one of these." She rested a hand on her pregnant belly and laughed.

I joined in. It was good to start the day with some fun.

Then Sam texted, confirming that he was coming to my house on Saturday afternoon for a bit of historical detective work before my parents arrived. I told him how eager I was to see him, and I got his assurance that he wouldn't mention the murder case to my mom and dad. They'd been so worried when I got involved in investigating crimes before. No need to concern them now.

The rest of my Friday was much less enjoyable, a frenzy of revising and polishing the grant proposal. Finally, ten minutes before the five o'clock deadline, I submitted it electronically. I'd cut it close, but at last it was done.

That evening I switched from cleaning up the proposal to cleaning up my apartment in preparation for my parents' visit. First, I brushed Bella until her coat gleamed. She loved being brushed, and spending time with her was a great way to unwind after my work week.

Then I put my favorite Steely Dan album on the turntable my dad had in college, and I worked on my apartment. Bella supervised. I scrubbed. I vacuumed. I rearranged my living room furniture and moved it back to the way I'd had it before. Saturday morning, I even ran to the store and bought an inexpensive fall bouquet and some scented candles, which I burned for an hour to make the whole apartment smell like apple cider and cinnamon.

After my divorce and job loss in Philadelphia, I wanted my parents to see that I was doing just fine, making a new life for myself in Dogwood Springs.

Saturday afternoon, right when Sam had said he'd come by, there was a knock on the door to my apartment.

Bella ran over, and I hurried after her to open the door.

She surged into the entryway, circling Sam and letting out happy barks.

"Quite the welcome." Sam led Bella into my apartment, rubbed her belly when she flopped on her back, and told her he'd missed her.

"I think she's glad to see you." I grinned at the two of them.

"Yep. I think so." Sam stood back up, took my hand and gazed at me for a long moment, then drew me into his arms and spoke more softly. "And I'm very glad to see you."

I looked back at him, my heart as warm and gooey as the inside of a toasted marshmallow. For a man I'd only met five months ago, he sure felt important to me.

"I'm glad to see you too." I wrapped my arms around his waist and pulled him closer.

"I can't believe I had to grade all last weekend. These extra classes I'm teaching are seriously getting in the way." He trailed a finger down my cheek. "We need a lot more time to ... figure out what happened to Ivy." His eyes met mine, and he leaned down and kissed me.

Warmth swirled through my chest, and thoughts of Ivy evaporated from my mind.

At last, we both stepped back, breathless.

I swallowed. "I, uh, I guess we'd better take a look at the Missouri Digital Newspaper Project to see if we can find Ivy's obituary. It would have more information than a death record."

"There's a Missouri Digital Newspaper Project?"

I picked up my laptop from my dining table and sat down next to Sam on the couch. "There sure is. Thanks to the efforts of groups like the Missouri Press Association and the State Historical Society, now that we know when Ivy died, I think we'll easily be able to find Ivy's obituary online."

Bella rubbed her head against Sam's leg.

He petted her while I started up my laptop.

Eventually, she went across the room and returned to lie at his feet with her favorite toy, a stuffed chicken.

It only took a few minutes for me to find the scanned pages of the *Silersville Gazette* from 1905.

"Silersville," Sam said. "That was the original name of Dogwood Springs, right?"

"It sure was. Until Great-Great-Grandma Elsie convinced the town to change it." I opened the website to the first page of the issue that came out right after Ivy died. The newspaper was pretty much what I expected with seven narrow columns of type on each page, divided by thin lines. There were no photographs but, unlike most papers today, there were ads on the front page, some of which included line drawings. I slowly flipped through the four-page weekly.

"Finally, the local news." Sam pointed at the screen. "On the back page."

Tucked next to a notice about a new blacksmith shop and an ad for binder twine, we found one obituary. But it wasn't for Ivy. It was for a 48-year-old woman, the mother of ten children, four of whom were living.

"Maybe it's in the next edition." I clicked back a screen and chose the back page of the next edition.

After a few seconds scanning the screen, Sam stiffened.

"Look." He pointed at an item several paragraphs long. "She was murdered."

I gasped. "Murdered?" I leaned in and read the article.

BANK ROBBERY AND FATAL SHOOTING

Miss Ivy Whitfield, aged eighteen years, daughter of Horace Whitfield and the late Mary Whitfield, was killed Sunday evening while putting an emerald necklace in the vault at the Silersville State Bank, which is owned by her father.

Because the sound of the gunfire was masked by a loud thunderstorm, the crime was not immediately discovered. As the evening grew later, Mr. Whitfield became concerned by his daughter's delay in returning home. He went to the bank and discovered her body. Distraught, and realizing that nothing could help his poor daughter, he immediately contacted his brother-in-law, Mr. Oliver Ferris of the Ferris Funeral Home.

Mr. Ferris removed the body and then, steeled by his profession to be clear-headed in times of crisis, recognized that the culprit might still be in the area. The sheriff was called, and the fire bell was rung to sound the alarm. Despite a lengthy search of the city and county by squads of armed men, the gunman escaped.

The culprit took the emerald necklace as well as a large sum of money from the vault. The necklace had been an engagement present from Miss Whitfield's fiancé, Willard Fore.

Miss Whitfield was considered an exemplary young

woman and will be sorely missed by her father, her step-mother, Blanche Ferris Whitfield, her half sister, Florence Whitfield, and her fiancé. Her remains were laid to rest in a private ceremony at the Silersville Cemetery.

The whereabouts of the killer are unknown. Authorities say the chances of recovering the money from the vault and the necklace are slim.

Chills went down my spine. "How horrible. She died simply because she was at the wrong place at the wrong time."

"You were right, though." Sam pointed to the screen. "Mary was her mother, and Blanche was her stepmother."

I rubbed the back of my neck, thinking. The painting still didn't make sense to me. "If she died in such a tragic event, why would anyone paint her out of the family portrait?"

"I don't know." Sam leaned in to read the screen again. "Maybe it was like the art restorer theorized. Maybe someone—like the half sister—hated her and had her painted out after the parents died."

"That's pretty mean. And this is so frustrating. I had hoped there would be more information, and I don't know what we do now."

"Now we wait for your parents to get here and go have dinner. I have full confidence that you, with your historic sleuthing skills, will figure out a way we can learn more about Ivy."

"I hope so." I closed the laptop. "Or maybe Rodney will know something."

Sam took my hand and gave it a squeeze. "One thing I've learned in dealing with computer problems is to trust my subconscious. The answer will come percolating up if you give it time. And if you administer carbs."

"Good thing we're going to La Villetta. Pasta should do the trick."

"They're here!" I pointed out my living room window at a burgundy SUV pulling up in front of the house.

Sam and Bella and I hurried outside. I was nervous about introducing my parents to Sam, but even more excited about having them visit.

I hadn't seen my parents since I moved to Dogwood Springs five months ago, but they hadn't changed a bit.

They parked on the street as I'd suggested, and Dad climbed out first. His blue eyes crinkled, and his smile spread, showing his dentist-perfect teeth. He had short, sandy-brown hair that was graying at the temples, and he stayed very fit with a five-mile run several times a week. He walked around the car and pulled me into a big hug.

Mom quickly joined us, looking exactly like me, or what I'd look like in thirty years. Big green eyes, narrow face, and a wide smile. She wore her hair shorter than mine, in a chin-length bob with bangs, and a few years back had allowed it to go salt-and-pepper gray. Her eyes shone as she pulled me close.

I introduced Sam, and my parents quickly told him to call them Pam and Wayne. Then I introduced Bella, who charmed them immediately by tilting her head to one side, being adorable, and politely soaking up the attention as they patted her. I finished off the welcome with a tour of my apartment, even showing them Haunting Harold, who was still on display because Cleo was so fond of him.

Quickly, I realized that my fears had been foolish. Sam and my parents got along well, and despite my mom's tendency to be a bit free with her opinions on how other people should live their lives, she seemed to be on her best behavior.

We took two cars, and both found parking in the lot behind La Villetta. A few minutes later we were shown to our table. La Villetta's dining room was the fanciest in Dogwood Springs, and the food was so good that patrons came from not only the local area, but also from towns nearby like Westfield and Rolla.

Sparkling chandeliers and elaborate wall fixtures gleamed, a tall candle glowed on every table, and the smell of freshly baked bread made my mouth water. The formality of the white tablecloths and white cloth napkins was offset by a square of tan paper, the kind used for wrapping packages, that was laid at an angle across each table, with the corners curling down over the sides. Soft classical music played in the background, and conversations were fairly low, but the vibe was relaxed enough to accommodate a tourist who only packed jeans for their visit to Dogwood Springs or a table laughing loudly at a good joke.

And the menu…

I'd eaten food from La Villetta twice before. Once, when I was quite young at a family event and once when Sam had a special meal catered for the two of us. But now, seeing the list of pastas and specialty dishes, I realized choosing was going to be a challenge.

Eventually, I settled on ravioli filled with butternut squash and Roquefort cheese, covered in a rich cream sauce.

Once we'd ordered, and the server had left a basket of hot bread, I pulled a present from my big purse and handed it to my mom.

She tilted her head to one side. "What's this?"

"You'll just have to open it and see." I grinned at Sam.

Mom ripped off the paper, and a smile spread across her face. Apparently, my gift of a signed copy of *One Woman's Legacy*, a book a Grove University professor had recently published about Mom's great-grandmother, Elsie Dorsett, was a hit.

Mom thanked me, hugged the book to her chest, and then tucked it into her purse, which was almost as big as mine, to make sure she didn't spill something on it. "What a lovely gift," she said. "Oh, and speaking of history, I have news."

Dad took a slice of bread, passed the basket to Sam, and gave us an I've-already-heard-this look.

Sam and I each took a slice of bread and added butter, then leaned in.

I took a bite. The bread was sourdough, and it tasted even better than it smelled.

"I talked to Gloria." My mom angled her head toward Sam. "My oldest sister, who you bought Ashlington from. I asked if she knew where that painting you found in the attic came from."

Sam's eyes narrowed. "I had asked her that in my email, but she said she didn't know."

Mom sniffed. "With Gloria, you have to give her time to think a bit. She's always been off in her own little world."

A nice way of putting it. Aunt Gloria was flat-out dingy.

"Anyway, she said she thinks our mom bought it at the Methodist church's fall bazaar back in the early 1970s. She remembers that our dad hated it, so it got stuck in the attic. And she had no idea who might have donated it to the bazaar."

My shoulders sank. "I can't imagine anyone at the church remembering who donated it at this point, although I guess we could ask." I explained to my parents what we'd learned about Ivy being murdered. My parents were surprised, but they didn't seem as fascinated with the story as Sam and me.

"I don't know, Libby." Mom slathered a thick layer of butter on a slice of sourdough. "Maybe you shouldn't worry about why that girl was painted out of the picture. It could be a big waste of time."

My chest tightened, and I fought to keep a pleasant

expression on my face. Really, if I wanted to waste my time, it was my own choice, wasn't it?

Sam squeezed my hand under the table. "I have to disagree, Pam. I've been so impressed with all the ways Libby knows to learn about things in the past. I bet in the end she figures this out."

Mom blinked a few times and nodded. "You may be right."

Dad looked over at Sam, then caught my eye and winked at me. My date had just scored big points in Dad's book.

Our salads arrived, and Dad entertained us with a story of a pair of six-year-old identical twins who had visited the office on Halloween, each dressed as a tooth. They had proudly told him how to tell the two of them apart. One was a molar, the other an incisor.

After that, the meal continued to go smoothly. Mom, Dad, and Sam all loved their entrees, and the dish I'd ordered was fantastic. The tender pillows of pasta were practically bursting with the contrasting flavors of the sweet butternut squash and the tangy cheese, and the cream sauce was exceptional. Truly, the meal was as good as any I'd eaten when my ex-husband had taken me to the finest restaurant in Philadelphia for our anniversary. One more reason to love living in Dogwood Springs.

After we ordered dessert, I slipped away to use the restroom.

When I came back, Sam's posture seemed rigid, and Dad looked at me as if he'd just learned that I had a cavity.

Nerves twitched in my stomach. "What's going on?" I slid into my chair and glanced at Sam. Had he somehow mentioned that I'd gotten involved in another mystery?

"Nothing, dear." Mom scooped up the last bite of her chocolate mousse. "I was just telling Dad and Sam that they should have ordered this. It's amazing."

Ahh. I relaxed. No mention of my sleuthing. And my mom wasn't telling people how to live their entire lives, just what they should eat. "To each their own," I said.

Once we finished our meal, Mom and Dad headed to the B & B.

Sam and I waved goodbye, and then I caught his arm. "I'm sorry about my mom. I should have warned you that she'd try to tell you what dessert to order, how to vote, and what you should choose for a career."

He brushed my comment aside as we got into his car. "I have a great-aunt who does the same thing. I know Aunt Della and your mom mean well. They think they're helping."

I let out a sigh and nodded. "It's not always helpful, though."

"Don't worry about it." Sam started the engine. "I feel very confident in my choice of Dutch apple pie with ice cream, who I voted for, and my career choices."

"Good." I sank back into the seat. He drove me home, and we decided to make an early evening of it since I was getting up extra early the next day for breakfast with my parents.

After he left, though, I realized that our goodnight kiss hadn't given me the same zing as it usually did.

That's what stress could do to a person. Maybe I'd been more nervous about dinner with my parents than I'd realized.

Despite my worry, though, I'd survived the meal. And Sam and I hadn't figured out why Ivy was painted out of the portrait, but I wasn't giving up. Especially not after he said he believed in me.

Chapter Fifteen

SUNDAY MORNING, Mom and Dad knocked on my door at six thirty, all packed up and checked out of the B & B. Although Mom's friend who owned the Hilltop Bed and Breakfast made a fabulous breakfast spread, on Sundays it didn't start until eight, and my parents had plans for lunch with friends in Kansas City, which was three and a half hours away. The Dogwood Café, which opened early every day, was the answer.

They sat on the couch for a few minutes with Bella on the floor between them, getting attention from one of them and then the next. After Bella had convinced them both that she was the sweetest dog ever, the three of us went to the café, leaving her at home since the outdoor tables had been closed for the winter.

Inside, the café was warm and cozy with walls the color of hot cocoa and highly polished wooden tables. The clinking of silverware and the hum of conversation filled the air, along with the rich aroma of coffee. Even though I'd never learned to enjoy the taste of coffee, the smell conjured up memories of warm hugs from my parents first thing in the morning and always made me happy.

Marcus seated us, the three of us ordered pancakes, and Dad told me their vacation itinerary in detail. A stop in Kansas City to see old friends, an overnight visit in Kansas to see his sister and her husband, more than a week in Colorado at some fossil-hunting sites, and then a drive to Lincoln, Nebraska, where Dad had a dental conference. To me, the four days at the conference sounded a bit dull for Mom, but she was eager to attend, saying that many of the same spouses were at the conference every year, and she looked forward to seeing them.

As we were buttering our pancakes, Dad looked over at me. "Was everything all right with Sam after dinner last night?"

"Yes, all is good." Count on Dad to pick up on Mom's less than tactful comments telling Sam what he should eat.

Dad's shoulders eased, and he poured maple syrup over his blueberry-banana pancakes. "Great. He seems like a good guy."

At one point, Mom tried to tell me that I should go back to wearing bangs, but I rolled my eyes and reminded her that I was thirty-two years old and could choose my own hairstyle. "Besides," I said, "my best friend, Cleo, who lives upstairs, is the best hairstylist in town. Trained in New York. She's in charge of my hair."

Mom shrugged and admitted that the color did look nice.

I took that as a major victory and switched the subject to my brother's kids, a topic both my parents could happily discuss for hours.

They drove me back to my place, hugged me repeatedly, and headed off to Kansas City.

I went inside, collapsed on the couch, and considered the visit a success. I texted Sam, Cleo, Alice, and Zeke and invited them over after dinner to discuss the case. Sam sent his regrets. He had sixty-five exams to grade for one of Professor Brown's classes by the next morning, each with six complicated problems. He said he'd spend hours giving partial credit. The next two nights, he added, he'd be writing an exam for one of his own classes. Teaching a double load did not sound fun.

Thankfully, my other three friends were available.

Maybe if the four of us worked together, we could figure out what to do next in our investigation.

That afternoon, Bella and I went on a long walk, and I did two loads of laundry and my weekly shopping, where I stocked up on essentials like shortbread cookies. By seven, when everyone was due to arrive, I felt ready to face the new work week.

The doorbell rang, and Bella raced to the door.

Cleo came down the stairs and joined me in greeting Alice, who carried a clear plastic food storage container.

Cleo's eyes lit and she pointed to the container. "What's in there?"

"Chocolate cupcakes that I made for a Halloween event at church." Alice walked across my living room and set the container on my dining table. "I gave some away at the end of the event, but I brought the rest of the leftovers home, thinking I'd give them to my daughter and the kids." She took off the lid.

Cleo and I peered in.

"They're adorable!" Cleo rested a hand on Alice's shoulder.

She was right. Some of the cupcakes were decorated as pumpkins with a big swirl of orange frosting on top, a small green frosting stem, and candy eyes. The rest were cupcake mummies, with strips of white frosting bandaging a chocolate face with candy eyes peeking out.

"Your grandsons didn't want them?" I'd have thought any three-year-old would be thrilled to eat them. "They look yummy." Since Alice had made them, I was sure they were.

Alice rolled her eyes. "After Halloween, my daughter decided that the boys need to eat fewer sweets. She thinks less sugar will make them less rowdy. I think rowdy is pretty much to be expected with twin boys that are almost four, but maybe she has a point." Alice gestured to the cupcakes. "Anyway, I thought perhaps you all might like some."

We assured her that she was right.

Alice tipped her head to one side. "And Zeke..."

Cleo laughed. "Alice, if you let him, I'm sure Zeke could eat the whole container, all"—she ran a finger over the air above the cupcakes—"fourteen of them."

"And never gain an ounce," I said.

A knock came at the door, and Bella and I let Zeke in.

His eyes lit when he heard about the cupcakes, and he quickly set down his backpack by the front door.

I collected plates, napkins, and drinks from the kitchen, and the four of us wasted no time in serving ourselves. I took a mummy cupcake. Cleo and Alice each had a pumpkin cupcake, and after encouragement from Alice, Zeke put one of each on his plate.

Bella sniffed near the table, but I told her that chocolate wasn't safe for dogs. I pushed the container to the middle of the table to be sure she didn't try to sneak one and gave her a dog biscuit.

We settled in the living room with Bella crunching loudly, and I peeled the paper off my cupcake. "Zeke, did you learn anything about Marla?"

He paused, half-eaten cupcake partway to his mouth, orange frosting on his chin. "Everything on her social media seems legit. From what I can tell, she really is visiting family in Texas."

"Thanks for checking that out. It seems like we can scratch her off our list of suspects." I took a big bite of cupcake. I was right. They were delicious. The cupcakes were dense and fudgy, and the frosting was buttercream, both clearly homemade.

Cleo set her half-eaten cupcake on her plate. "I've got a major clue." She sat up taller on the couch. "Right before I came downstairs, Freddie, Monica and Gary Boyd's assistant, sent me a message through the salon's website, asking me to call him. Well, actually, he sent the message late last night, but I didn't see it until today."

I licked a glob of frosting off my finger. "And?"

"He heard the whole conversation between us and Monica. He says that if she wants privacy, simply shutting her office door isn't enough. She needs to not talk so loudly. Although I wouldn't put it past him to have been listening at the door." Cleo chuckled. "Anyway, remember how Monica told us that she was planning to break up with Karl?"

I wiped my finger on my napkin. "I remember."

"Big. Fat. Lie." Cleo leaned back and looked around, as if making sure we were listening. "She was devastated when Karl started talking about seeing other people. Freddie heard her telling a friend on the phone."

"Oooh." Alice tapped one finger on the table. "That is interesting."

"Could be a motive for murder," Zeke said. "The woman scorned."

Cleo beamed at him like a proud parent. "And"—she paused dramatically—"Monica wasn't in the office the whole afternoon the day that Karl was murdered like she said she was. According to Freddie, about two o'clock that day, he managed to drag himself to the pharmacy to get something for his fever. He saw Monica driving toward Karl's house."

"Very interesting. So she had motive and opportunity." I ate the last bite of my cupcake, sat for a moment, and decided that more chocolate would probably enhance my sleuthing skills. I got up, put a cupcake decorated as a pumpkin on my plate, and sat back down.

Zeke, I noticed, had already finished both of his cupcakes, but didn't go back for more.

I angled my head toward the dining area and looked at him. "Want another?"

He shook his head. "I've got the PSAT tomorrow, and I'm already feeling queasy about it."

Cleo's eyes widened. "Buddy, you can't possibly be worried. You'll ace it, no problem."

"I hope so." Zeke picked at a frayed place on his jeans. "I need to do well enough to get a scholarship that will convince my dad to let me go to school where I want, not where I can pledge his old fraternity."

I added my assurances, but my words didn't seem to have much effect.

Alice leaned in. "Zeke, you're one of the brightest kids to go through the Dogwood Springs schools in years. I'm almost certain this test will show that," she said gently. "But if it doesn't, you have other indicators that demonstrate what a success you'll be in college. Truly, you're going to have more opportunities than you know what to do with."

As she spoke, tension fell from Zeke's face and posture. His shoulders and even his hands grew more relaxed. Count on Alice to know exactly what to say.

"Thanks." His head tipped to one side. "Did they have the PSAT when you were in high school?"

She laughed. "They did, but it didn't matter for me. I started working at the grocery store when I was sixteen and stayed there until I got married." She paused. "I kind of regret that these days. It seems like everyone I know has at least one degree."

I looked over at her, thinking of all the work she did flawlessly as a volunteer for the museum. "I never realized you didn't have a degree, Alice. I don't care in the least, and I imagine no one else does either."

She gave an unconvincing smile. "Nothing to worry about. What we need to do is solve this crime." Her eyes narrowed. "Let's assume Monica knew about Karl's love of caramel truffles and wanted to kill him. Would she have access to sleeping pills and know how many to use?"

"She could find that information on the Internet," Zeke said. "And she could buy the pills online if she knew where to look."

"Or..." I thought a moment as I unwrapped my second cupcake, being careful not to mess up the frosting. "If she has access to people's homes when she's decorating, she could steal them from someone's medicine cabinet."

Cleo nodded vigorously, her mouth full of cupcake. She held up a finger and swallowed. "So that gives her motive, means, and opportunity."

"If she is the killer, all we need is a way to trick her into confessing." I polished off my second cupcake, wondering how we could make that happen.

The next morning I started my work week by giving a presentation to a local seniors' organization about some fascinating homes, now torn down, that had once been a part of Dogwood Springs.

I concluded with a pitch for the historic homes tour. The audience was incredibly receptive. Almost every person bought at least one ticket for the tour, exactly what I'd been hoping for. The closer we got to the event, the more urgency I felt about making it a success so we could pay for the new HVAC system.

I finished my presentation at eleven thirty and decided, since I was already out, to head home for an early lunch. I had just filled Bella's food bowl and was rummaging through the refrigerator when footsteps pounded down the front stairs and someone banged on my door.

Bella galloped into the living room with me at her heels.

"Libby!" Cleo shouted through the door.

My heart sped. What was going on? I unlocked the door and opened it.

"I've been texting you and texting you."

I waved her inside and glanced at my purse, where my phone was. "I'm sorry. I gave a presentation to a seniors' group this morning and turned my volume off. What's going on?"

"You're never going to believe this." Her words tumbled out. "Monica's dead."

Chapter Sixteen

"DEAD?" I couldn't believe it. Monica had been our chief suspect.

Cleo nodded.

Bella looked up at Cleo expectantly until she scratched Bella's ears.

"Come into the kitchen." I led the way. "Have you eaten?"

"No, since I'm off today, I'm meeting my mom for lunch."

"Do you have time to tell me what you know?" I pulled a prepared meal from my freezer and stuck it in the microwave.

"I've got time." Cleo leaned back against the counter. "Freddie took time off first thing this morning to go get his eyes checked. When he came to work about ten, Monica was at her desk, dead."

"How did you find out?"

"He texted me. He thinks you and Alice and Zeke and me are far more likely to figure out who killed her than the police are."

"They're sure it was murder?"

"From what Freddie heard from the officers, they don't know. But he thinks it's just too much of a coincidence."

The microwave dinged. I peeled back the plastic wrap, stirred my lunch, and stuck it back in for another two minutes. "I agree with him. It does seem like too much of a coincidence."

Cleo checked the clock on my stove and moved toward the door to the living room. "I'd better run if I'm going to meet my mom. But I wanted you to know."

"Thanks. This is a big deal. We've clearly been looking at this all wrong." I got a can of soda out of the fridge. "Are you free for dinner tonight? I think we should get together with Alice and Zeke if they're available and figure out what to do next."

"Definitely," Cleo said. "I bet they're both free. I think Alice's husband is out of town for the next two weeks on business, and I know my sister-in-law has a club meeting tonight. Zeke will be happy not to eat my brother's cooking." She hesitated. "What about Sam?"

"He's still swamped. Writing an exam tonight."

Cleo gave Bella a quick pat and stepped toward the door. "I'll see if Freddie learns anything more from the police."

~

By five o'clock, the weather had turned, and I'd been so busy thinking of Monica's death that I hadn't even considered taking my car or an umbrella to work after lunch.

All the way home, icy rain poured down, and the wind had to be at least twenty miles an hour. By the time I got inside, I was soaked, frozen, and miserable, suddenly panicked that the weather on the day of the homes tour might be equally nasty. I could only imagine how unhappy the homeowners would be if the tour groups tracked mud through their houses.

I quickly changed into dry clothes, wrung out my hair, and brushed it. Then I let Bella out and stood in my rain slicker under Cleo's deck. If I positioned myself right, away from the areas where water ran off in a stream, the porch offered enough protection for me to check the long-range weather forecast on my phone. According to the meteorologists, Saturday, November 18, would be sunny with a high of 53.

That was twelve days away, beyond the point where I trusted them, but I sure hoped they were right.

Bella didn't enjoy the rain any more than I did, and we were soon back inside where I dried her off and wiped the mud from her feet.

I filled her food bowl, then I blow-dried my hair and drove downtown to the café. One trip walking in that rain was enough.

From the availability of parking downtown, it looked as if the tourists were staying in, perhaps having food delivered to their rooms at the local B & Bs. I found a spot in the same block as the café, and I parked and hurried toward the door, trying to hold off the rain by keeping my umbrella practically sideways.

Inside, the café was less crowded than usual, but—maybe because it was so cold and wet outside—it felt extra cozy. The rich scent of coffee and fried onions wrapped around me like a hug.

Alice and Cleo waved from a table in the far corner, well away from the door. Zeke sat facing me with his head buried in a menu.

"I'm sorry," I said as I sat down in my regular seat. "I got soaked going home to let Bella out, and I had to dry my hair. I was frozen." Even now, I felt cold, and I kept my coat around my shoulders.

"We just sat down," Alice said. "Let's order, though. I've got news."

Cleo grabbed a menu. "Me too."

"I know what I want," Zeke said, closing his menu. "Today's special is a Philly cheese steak with fried onions, French fries, and coleslaw."

The rest of us exchanged glances.

"That sounds perfect." Cleo shut her menu.

I didn't even bother picking one up. "I don't know how I could order anything else after smelling those onions." Especially with the added attraction of the café's coleslaw, a local favorite.

The server came over and we all ordered the special, even Alice, although she mumbled something about fat grams. Perhaps, as my mother said, turning fifty really did wreak havoc on a woman's metabolism.

Finally warm, I pushed my coat over the back of my chair. "Okay, team, what have you got?"

Cleo sat up taller. "I talked to Freddie, who overheard two officers when he had to fill out paperwork at the police station. They think Monica might have been poisoned with sleeping pills like Karl, then smothered."

"Have they already gotten a toxicology report?" Zeke asked.

"I don't think so, but apparently there were no indications that she'd tried to defend herself, so they think the killer somehow incapacitated her."

"I have worse news," Alice said. "Gail's been arrested."

"Wow." No matter how hard I tried, I couldn't picture Gail smothering Monica. I started to ask a question about Gail, but I spotted our server coming toward us with a tray of drinks. I angled my head in his direction.

The others caught my meaning, and Cleo quietly told us about a crochet project she was considering and all of us—even Zeke—listened as if we were fascinated.

The server set down coffee for Cleo and Alice, a soda for Zeke, and a mug of hot tea for me.

As soon as the server had moved on, Cleo abandoned her description of yarn. "Listen to this. The client who told me this is a terrible gossip, and I normally don't put a lot of stock in what he tells me, but he says Gail was overheard asking a pharmacist about sleeping pills."

"So she could have been lying to us all along," Zeke said.

"She may have killed her husband and just be hoping we find someone else to blame."

"We do have to consider Gail," I said. "But I trust Alice's judgment of character. If she says Gail is innocent, I expect she's right."

"I am," Alice said. "Gail Wellston is no killer."

That was what my gut told me. Just like it told me that we were dealing with one killer, not two. I took a quick sip of tea and instantly regretted it. I didn't burn my tongue too badly, but it was still better to hold the mug than to actually drink from it. "Which means the police have arrested the wrong person and the real killer is still out there."

"And we have no way of knowing who they might murder next," Zeke said.

My stomach tightened. Perhaps partly in denial, I'd been thinking of the killer's motivation as personal and believing that unless I was obvious in my sleuthing, I was safe. But if someone had already killed twice, they'd have little difficulty killing again. Anyone who'd seen something or overheard something or looked at the killer the wrong way could possibly be next. "You're right, Zeke. This isn't only about justice for Karl and protecting Gail, it's about the safety of the whole community."

"So how do we figure this out?" Alice asked.

I sat my tea mug down with a clunk. "We have to dig deeper. One of our suspects must be hiding something."

Alice nodded.

I leaned in. "Gary is a strong suspect. He could have

killed both Karl and Monica because he was upset about the affair. And we can't rule out Cheryl or Amber or Dr. Roth. Any one of them could have been lying too. We're pretty much back where we started, except that we ruled out Marla, and we can't consider Monica a suspect anymore."

"So, five suspects?" Cleo said.

"Five." I agreed. "Gail and Gary, both wronged spouses because of the affair. Cheryl because of her sister's death. Amber because she was fired. And Dr. Roth over how much he got paid at the medical practice."

"Time to get back to sleuthing," Cleo said.

"It is." I took a sip of tea, which had finally cooled enough to drink.

Alice worried her lower lip and looked at me. "I hate to say this, Libby, but if we don't solve this soon, and we believe the real killer is still out there, you and I may have to talk to the board."

My stomach sank as I realized what she was going to say. "We may have to cancel the homes tour?"

"It wouldn't be responsible to hold a special event drawing people to the area, if there's a killer out there—a killer who's already murdered a homeowner and a decorator that were both connected to the tour."

"Maybe we could simply postpone it?" I tried to keep the disappointment out of my voice but failed.

"Possibly," Alice said. "But the closer we get to Christmas, the harder it will be to find an open Saturday."

I let out a long sigh and stared at my mug.

After a minute, though, I raised my chin. "We can't give up. This is just one more reason we need to find the killer. To ensure that we can have the homes tour, to keep Gail out of jail, to find justice for Karl and Monica, and, most importantly, to keep the community safe."

Chapter Seventeen

MONDAY NIGHT, the temperature dropped below freezing.

When I got to the museum at nine on Tuesday morning, the temperature inside was a chilly 49 degrees. The next few days were supposed to be much warmer, but I knew the building would take time to heat back up. Today and tomorrow, the museum would be too cold for staff or visitors.

I checked with the HVAC service, who apologized profusely but said there had been an emergency at a local school. They couldn't work at the museum until they got the elementary kids back in their building, which would take a minimum of two days. So I had Imani put a notice on our website that we would be closed for two days, I put a sign on the front door, and I asked Rodney and Imani to work from home. I rescheduled a visit from a potential donor and collected files to take home.

As I closed my office door, I noticed the box with the mystery item that Imani had set on my desk. She and I could savor our victory in Rodney's game another time. When the museum didn't feel like the inside of a refrigerator.

What with shifting to working from home on Tuesday, sleuthing barely crossed my mind. I set up shop on my dining table, actually got a lot done, and enjoyed spending the day with Bella. For her part, she loved having me home. If she could talk, I had a suspicion she'd recommend I stop going into the museum completely.

On Wednesday, Alice called and said Gail was out on bail. She suggested the two of us talk with her once more.

I agreed, and Wednesday, after a quick dinner, I met Alice outside the Wellstons' home.

We climbed the front stairs, Alice knocked, and Gail let us in and led us, like before, to the kitchen.

The room was the same—still a sunny yellow with white cabinets, white marble counters, and an easy-to-live-in style. And the house was quiet in a way that my apartment, with its single-pane windows and location on a busier street, could never be. But the kitchen smelled like garbage that needed to be taken out.

And although it had been less than two weeks since I'd seen Gail, she appeared to have aged ten years. Her short, plain hair hung limp and had grown out just enough to expose roots that needed a touch-up. The lines around her mouth and between her eyebrows had deepened. And her skin had broken out, erupting in a large pimple on her chin that she picked at as she waved us toward the kitchen table.

Any confidence she had felt that someone other than

her would be convicted of Karl's murder was gone. She sank into one of the kitchen chairs, head drooping.

Alice quickly sat down and took Gail's hand. "We're here," she said. "And we believe you're innocent. We're hoping you can help us prove that to the police."

Gail sat up slightly and, with what appeared to be great effort, gave Alice a brave smile.

I didn't want to be mean, but I leaned forward, both elbows on the table and narrowed my eyes at her. "We do need the truth, though, Gail. The whole truth. Did you know about Karl's affair? And did you talk with a pharmacist about sleeping pills?"

She shrank back, hunkering down into her previous position. "I did know about the affair. I've known about all of his affairs, I think. But I never talked with anyone about sleeping pills." She glanced over at me. "You probably can't understand, but I didn't want a divorce. I didn't kill him. I simply wanted him to stop sleeping around. We had something once. I think… I think I was too demoralized to see a way to a better future. The only hope I had was to recreate the past."

I tamped down memories of my ex-husband. Being demoralized by infidelity was something I understood all too well, but I wanted to be sure she wasn't lying again. "No conversation with a pharmacist?"

"None, I swear. Someone is starting these rumors to try to make me look guilty, just like they planted those pills in my house. I can see why the police would think I killed Karl. He cheated on me. And"—her jaw tightened as if she was pressing her teeth together—"in a lot of other ways, he didn't treat me like I mattered. But I didn't kill him."

"I can see why the police believe you left the poisoned candy on the table before you went to the office," Alice said. "It would have been easier for you than for anyone else. Still, I think they need to look for a less obvious suspect."

"I'll tell you what I told my lawyer," Gail said. "I didn't poison any candy. There wasn't even any candy here when I left for work because Karl was trying to lose weight. His blood pressure had been creeping up. He hadn't bought any truffles in weeks."

I pushed my hair back. "They could say you poisoned some candy that had been in the house from before."

Gail gave a laugh that sounded as if she was choking. "Not if they knew Karl. If there were caramel truffles in the house, he ate them. Ask Mimi, at the candy shop. I've heard him tell her that a thousand times. And she can verify that I haven't been in the store in months."

I looked over at Alice. "I know the candy shop gets a ton of business, but it might be worth asking Mimi if she remembers who has bought caramel truffles."

Alice nodded.

The tiniest flicker of hope crossed Gail's eyes. "Thank you. I feel better with you trying to help. My lawyer says he'll get the case dismissed, but I don't see how."

Alice and I said our goodbyes, and I assured Alice I'd stop by the candy store the next day. Maybe we would get lucky. Maybe Mimi would verify that Gail hadn't bought any caramel truffles and say she'd sold several to one of our other suspects.

Thursday morning as I was getting dressed, the HVAC service called. If I could unlock the museum in half an hour, they would get started.

I scrambled to get ready as fast as possible, then raced to work, arriving just as the service truck pulled into the parking lot.

Inside the building that morning, it was cold, but not quite as cold as Tuesday. Imani, Rodney, and the volunteers seemed to take the slightly icy building in stride. Heat was coming.

At lunch I hurried home, fed Bella, and ate some left-over soft tacos. Even reheated, Mexican food was my favorite. Then I walked back downtown, stopping at Mimi's Candies.

Mimi's was a favorite of both tourists and locals alike, not only the source of all sorts of delicious treats, but darling as well. The awning of the shop was decorated to match Mimi's candy boxes, pink with a chocolate-brown ribbon and bow.

I opened the door, and a bell jangled. I inhaled deeply, drawing in the intoxicating aroma of chocolate, chocolate, and more chocolate.

The shop had high ceilings, lots of windows, and plants tucked in windowsills and niches, trailing down over the white walls. Display cases held handmade gourmet chocolates, and long tables covered in pink tablecloths held baskets filled with other candies. Behind the counter, a large green double door topped by an arched window led to the back, the magical world where the handmade candies were created.

Behind the counter, a young woman with a short blond ponytail with a cobalt-blue streak turned toward me. "Can I help you?"

"I was hoping to talk to Mimi, if she's available."

"Just a minute." The woman ducked through the green double doors, leaving me alone to stare at the chocolates in the case.

I'd first visited Mimi's when I came to town for my job interview and sometimes popped in on my way home from work, allowing myself a treat after a tough day.

Shortbread, of course, was my favorite sweet, but chocolate was practically medicinal, right? I was especially fond of the milk-chocolate-covered toffee.

I was just checking to see if any were in the case when the young woman returned, followed by Mimi.

"Libby." Her eyes lit. "How nice to see you. Dani said you had a question for me?"

Mimi was a tall, vivacious woman who I'd guess was in her early sixties. She wore her short blond hair standing almost straight up on top in a style that—though I'd never tell her—made her resemble a cotton swab. She had large, extra-white teeth, wore lipstick the same shade of pink as her candy boxes, and laughed a lot.

"Thanks for coming out from the kitchen. I did have a question." I moved closer, meeting her near the cash register. "I don't know if you heard, but Gail Wellston has been arrested for her husband's murder."

Mimi gave the most dramatic eye roll I'd ever seen. "I heard. I told John Harper it was ridiculous to suspect her. Gail probably feels guilty if she slaps a mosquito while it's biting her."

"She asked me to see if I could learn anything that would help her. And she said you might be able to corroborate that neither she nor her husband had bought any caramel truffles recently."

"I haven't sold them any," Mimi said. "Not since Karl came in the day of your birthday, Dani." Mimi waved over her assistant. "What day was that?"

"August twenty-seventh." Dani narrowed her eyes for a moment. "I don't think I've seen either of them in here since." Now that I looked at her more closely, I noticed how young she appeared. If it wasn't a school day, I'd have guessed she was still in high school.

"Those were definitely my truffles that the murderer used," Mimi said. "John brought one by." She pursed up her mouth. "I don't know why they had to involve my shop."

It had to have made Mimi's life harder, but I had to focus on the murder. "Gail swears that if they had caramel truffles in the house, Karl would have eaten them. Do you think that's accurate?"

Mimi looked me straight in the eye. "Meaning 'Do I

think Gail found some in the cabinet and poisoned them that morning?'"

I had been trying to be a little less obvious with my question, but she'd seen right through me. "Well, yeah."

"I can't imagine Karl letting caramel truffles lie around his house for more than a day. He admitted that he once ate four during a ten-minute drive home. So unless Gail planned this murder months in advance and had some secret hiding place, then no, I don't think she put out the poisoned truffles that morning." Mimi looked at me expectantly. "Who are your other suspects?"

"I hate to name names," I said. "They might be totally innocent."

"You're not telling me they're murderers. You're simply asking if they bought caramel truffles."

I tipped my head in acknowledgment. She seemed so confident that she'd know who'd bought truffles. I should have talked to her earlier. "Gary Boyd, the contractor. Cheryl Nichols, the landscaper. Amber Riley, a nurse, and Dr. Edward Roth, both from Karl's medical practice. And Marla, the Wellstons' housekeeper."

"Nope. Nope. Nope. Nope. And definitely not, I've never even seen her in the shop." Mimi frowned, as if realizing this made Gail seem more guilty. "What about you, Dani, have you sold caramel truffles to any of those people lately?"

Dani's face clouded. "I'm really sorry, but I don't know any of those people. I only know Dr. and Mrs. Wellston because he was my doctor, and she always says hi to me when I go in for my weekly allergy shots."

"I forgot," Mimi said. "You haven't lived in Dogwood Springs forever like I have."

"I'm sorry I'm not more help," Dani said.

"Would you remember them if I showed you a photo?" I pulled out my phone. I could find photos of some of our suspects online.

Dani's face fell. "I really doubt it. We get so many tourists in here that I don't always pay attention to people's faces."

"Don't worry." Mimi patted Dani's arm. "It's actually good. It means any of those people could be the murderer instead of Gail." She looked back at me. "And we have sold quite a few caramel truffles lately. Although fewer than over the summer, but that's probably related to the number of tourists in town."

I thanked them both and bought two pieces of milk-chocolate-covered toffee, one for my dessert after supper and one to cheer me up on my way back to work.

Because other than most likely clearing Gail, who I hadn't strongly suspected, I was no closer to finding the killer.

Chapter Eighteen

BACK AT THE MUSEUM, the servicemen were hard at work. By midafternoon, warm air was flowing down from the vent in my office. Rodney, Imani, and I all tried to get things done, but we spent a lot of time popping into each other's offices, discussing how great the heat felt.

Once I started home, my mind returned to the case. If someone was planting rumors about Gail, it was probably the killer. Could Cleo's gossipy client remember who had told him that Gail was overheard talking to a pharmacist about sleeping pills? Since it was Thursday, Cleo probably wouldn't be home for a couple of hours, but I'd be sure to pop upstairs later and ask her to check.

And if Kiara's husband worked for Gary, could he verify Gary's alibi about being with his crew the whole day of the murder? That might be something I could find out now. I sped up and within minutes spotted Bella's face at my living room window.

She let out a loud woof as I unlocked the outer door and, when I opened the door to my apartment, greeted me as if I was the most important person in the whole world, which I guess to her I was.

"Oh, sweetie, you mean the world to me as well." I knelt and petted her, then let her out into the backyard for a few minutes.

I fixed her supper, which she'd taught me should always be served as soon after five o'clock as possible. While she ate, I changed into my tennis shoes, drank a quick mug of tea, and ate the piece of chocolate-covered toffee I'd been saving for dessert, the perfect snack to tide me over until I fixed my own dinner later.

"How about a walk in a different direction today?" I asked when she'd finished eating.

Different direction may have been foreign to her, but walk was a word she knew well. She nudged her leash off its hook in the kitchen and carried it to me in her mouth.

Once we were outside, she turned to go on our usual route down Elm toward Fifth Street and on to turn around at Thirteenth.

"Let's go this way today, Bella." I tugged on her leash, leading her the opposite way. If we took Second Street over a couple of blocks, we'd be at Kiara and Tony's Craftsman home, and I could ask Tony if Gary really was with him the whole day of the murder.

Ten minutes later we climbed the wide steps of the one-and-a-half story bungalow. The house was a soft, mossy green, with a gray roof and gorgeous wood trim stained a warm brown. A hay bale was angled at the foot of the porch steps, topped with three bright orange pumpkins and clusters of ears of colorful, ornamental corn. And even now, in early November, I could see that Tony and Kiara used their deep front porch. Wool plaid blankets lay rumpled on matching wooden deck chairs, as if they'd been hurriedly tossed off. A mug on a small table held what looked like an inch of cold coffee.

I was about to knock when a white sedan turned into the driveway and gave a short beep of its horn. Kiara waved and pointed to the detached garage behind the house.

Bella and I followed her there and reached the garage just as she climbed out of her car.

"How nice to see you, Libby." She looked down at Bella. "And what's your name?"

I introduced Bella, who waited until Kiara scratched her ears, then rubbed her head against Kiara's leg.

"You are a charmer, aren't you?" Kiara said to Bella, seeming unconcerned about dog hair on her pants. Then she looked up at me. "What brings you by?"

I explained that I lived fairly close, and that I was hoping to talk to her husband. "Gary Boyd told me he was working on a house with his crew the entire day of the murder. I wondered if Tony could verify that."

"He's picking up barbecue for our dinner, which might take a while, depending on when he called the order in. Let me text him." She gestured to her back door. "Would the two of you like to come in?"

Images of the interior of the Norton home flitted

through my mind. "We'd better not. I remember seeing your lovely miniature village of Dogwood Springs when I came over to talk with you about the tour."

The gift shop on Main Street sold miniature ceramic buildings that were replicas of the downtown shops and local landmarks, like a personalized Christmas village. I had started a collection but mine was still small, and I kept it on my mantel. Kiara had the entire collection spread out on the sides of her hearth.

I glanced down at Bella. "I'd hate for it to get hit by someone's tail."

"Let's go sit on the front porch then," Kiara said.

A couple of minutes later we were each seated in a chair on the porch with a wool blanket spread over our legs to keep us nice and snug. "Text is better, right?" She said as she pulled her phone out of her purse. "So that other people at the barbecue place don't hear the conversation?"

"I'd appreciate it. I hate to be responsible for making people think Gary's a murderer if he's completely innocent."

She nodded, and her thumbs flew over her phone.

While I waited, Bella laid her head on my knee. I rubbed her silky ears and gazed at the trees on Second Street, festive in their fall foliage. As on Elm Street, most of the trees were hard maples with striking red leaves. The house across from Kiara and Tony's though, also had a sweet gum with deep burgundy leaves and a pair of gingko trees, both a gorgeous gold.

A text whooshed out from Kiara's phone, followed almost immediately by a ding.

"Wow." Kiara sat her phone in her lap. "I don't know if I feel better or worse after learning this."

"What?"

"I can't believe I never thought to ask him. After Gail was arrested, I thought I'd misjudged her and that she really had killed Dr. Wellston. But Tony says Gary was gone for three hours the afternoon of the murder."

"So Gary lied. He doesn't have an alibi and could have planted the poisoned chocolates in the Wellstons' house. And he definitely has a motive. Once he knew that Karl and Monica were having an affair, Gary could have killed them both."

Kiara looked like she might be ill. "So this means there's a smaller chance that I work with a woman who's a murderer, but most likely my husband works for a man who killed two people?"

"We don't know that, of course," I said quickly. "It just means there's a chance."

"True." She didn't look convinced.

"I'm sorry." I rose from my chair and neatly folded the wool blanket. "I didn't mean to freak you out."

"No." She stood. "It's not you. I was already pretty freaked out at the thought of someone I worked with being killed. And when Monica died... I sure hope either you or the police figure out who the killer is soon."

"I'll do my best," I said.

"I really hope it's not Gary," Kiara said.

I jiggled Bella's leash, waved, and walked down the porch steps, not saying a word.

Because if I had to pick the most likely suspect, it was Gary.

Chapter Nineteen

FRIDAY MORNING WAS cold and wet, with winds that must have been rerouted from the North Pole. Rodney, Imani, and I spent the first half hour of the day discussing the homes tour, checking and rechecking the long-range forecast, and trying to convince each other that the day of the tour, only eight days away, would be warm and sunny.

Why on earth hadn't I planned the event for May?

Midmorning, I got a call from Cleo. She'd heard from Freddie, who said Gary had family in from out of town for Monica's funeral. He would be out of the office all day.

"Get this." Cleo paused dramatically. "Freddie just happened to find Gary's computer password, written on a sticky note attached to the underside of his computer monitor."

"He did?"

"He said he was dusting the office." Cleo chuckled.

She bemoaned the fact that she had to work all day, without even a lunch break, but passed along an invitation from Freddie. If I wanted to, I could stop by the office, and the two of us could search for clues on Gary's computer. If Gary had ordered sleeping pills online, there should be a trail.

The idea didn't sit well in my stomach. If Gary was the killer, someone needed to do something. Two people were already dead.

But if he wasn't the killer, I would be sneaking into the office of a man who had just lost his wife. And would I actually find anything? "Wouldn't Gary have gotten rid of any evidence on his computer? Thrown it in the trash?"

"Doesn't stuff stay in the trash on a computer for a while? Maybe you could still find it."

"Me?" I was competent on a computer, but no genius. "Maybe Sam could find deleted files, but Friday is the day he teaches all afternoon. How about Zeke?"

"Not available. I tried to convince Freddie that we should look at Gary's computer tonight," Cleo said. "But he says Gary might notice car lights or the sound of the vehicles. During the day, it's normal for there to be some traffic."

That made sense. "And you drove your car when we went there to see him. When we went to see Monica, I drove, but he was on a job site. So if Gary saw my car outside the office, he wouldn't recognize it." I ran a hand back and forth over my pearls. "I guess I could try."

Cleo gave me Freddie's number, and I texted him, accepting his invitation and setting a time to stop by.

At twelve fifteen, after I'd dashed home to let Bella out, I parked outside the little tan office building. I shot a glance at the main house and noticed several cars parked out front but saw no sign of Gary. And there should be no way he'd know that Freddie and I accessed his computer. Just the same, I kept my head down as I dashed past the row of rust-colored mums in black pots and slipped in the door. If Gary was the murderer, he'd already killed two people. I had no desire to convince him that I should be number three.

Freddie let out a dramatic sigh when I walked in. "Finally! It's been all I could do not to check Gary's computer alone, but I thought it would be better to wait. If there are two of us, one can keep a lookout." He tipped his head to one side and gave a wry smile. "If Gary isn't the killer, I don't want to lose my job here."

"That makes sense. Do you want to keep watch or check the computer?"

"I'll keep watch." Freddie left his desk and positioned himself by the door, which had a good view of the main house. "If I see Gary, I can slide behind my desk and stall him when he comes in, giving you time to turn off the computer. Then you can wander back down the hall and thank me for letting you use the restroom."

He'd clearly thought this through. "But why would I be here? Isn't there a way I can slip out the back?"

"No. I'd still have to explain your car." He scratched his jaw, and then his face lit. "I know! Gary has original blue-prints of the Wellston home that he used when he was working on the basement. Maybe you wanted to see those because of the homes tour?"

"Original blueprints? I would like to see those."

"Not a problem, once we solve this case, Nancy Drew." He pointed to Gary's office. "The door is unlocked, and the sticky note with the password is on the bottom of the monitor, kind of behind the manufacturer's logo."

"Okay. I assume those sleeping pills were bought in the past couple of months. I can search for files created after a certain date."

"Good idea." He made a shooing motion, sending me toward Gary's office.

I drew in a deep breath, entered Gary's office, and sat down behind the desk.

Just like when Cleo and I had been here talking with Gary, the office was extremely tidy with the few papers on the desk neatly stacked. Hopefully, his computer files would be as tidy.

I turned on the machine and the external monitor, then reached under the front of the monitor and found the note with the password.

Seriously? Why did he go to the bother of creating a nonsense password with all these random capital letters and punctuation if he was going to hide it in his office in a place so easy to—

A soft *clunk* sounded above me.

I leapt out of the chair.

There was a *whoosh*, and heat came flowing down from the vent above.

Strange how having the HVAC system be functional can be a wonderful experience in your own office and nearly scare you out of your skin when you're snooping in someone else's.

I sat back down and typed in the password.

"Anything?" Freddie called from the other room.

"Not yet. The computer's still booting up." Slowly. Very slowly. And all the while Gary could be deciding that in spite of the fact that he had family in town for his wife's funeral, he needed to stop by the office.

At last, the computer was ready, and Gary's electronic calendar popped up, as if he left it open all the time.

I ignored it and ran a search for files created in the past two months. One by one, I checked them. Receipts for supplies, project timelines, a letter to his accountant. Nothing about the man seemed suspicious.

Except, of course, the fact that he'd lied to Cleo and me about where he'd been the day of Karl's murder.

I ran a search for one month prior, but still found nothing. I even figured out how to look in his electronic trash can, but there was nothing of use there either.

With a heavy sigh, I began closing windows, until the calendar was back in view. I scanned November but found nothing of interest except the time for Monica's funeral and visitation, both to be held tomorrow.

On a whim, I flipped back to October.

My breath caught. Bingo. There, on Tuesday, October 24, the day of Karl's murder, was a note that said:

"IMPORTANT! COURT DATE. 1 P.M."

"Freddie," I yelled. "Come here!"

He scurried in, glanced back at the hall, then came to stand beside me. "What?

I pointed. "Gary couldn't have killed Karl. He was in court. I don't know why he didn't tell us that."

Freddie's blue eyes grew wide. "Oh, I bet I do. Gary—"

There was a rattle.

My blood froze.

Because it wasn't a rattle that sounded like the HVAC system. Or a rattle that sounded like a branch blowing against the outside of the building. No, this was a rattle that sounded like the front door opening.

I turned to look at Freddie, but he was gone. One second, he'd been beside me, the next I heard his footsteps walking down the hall.

My heart raced as I scrambled, switching the calendar back to November, shutting down the computer, sticking the note with the password under the edge of the monitor. I slipped out of the chair, eased it back into its neatly aligned position, and was about to dash across the hall to the bathroom when I heard Freddie in the lobby.

"Oh, thank you," he said loudly. "We've been expecting this delivery. Once again, Fed Ex came through for us."

My breath whooshed out, my heart rate dropped out of the red zone, and I sank down to sit on the edge of the desk.

Once I heard the delivery man tell Freddie goodbye and leave, I glanced around the office again, made sure everything appeared as it had when I came in, and walked back near Freddie's desk. "I think that took two years off my life."

Freddie fanned his face with one hand. "Mine too!"

"So what was Gary in court for? And why didn't he tell Cleo and me that was where he was?"

"If it was anything related to work, he'd have told me. So I bet it's the paternity thing."

"What paternity thing?"

"Well, I'm not supposed to know, but Gary learned he has a child from a relationship he was in before he married Monica. Gary and the mother were never married. I bet that's what he was in court for. The kid is six years old, and Gary never even knew he existed. The mom contacted him out of the blue wanting child support. I was kind of impressed at how he reacted. He was more than happy to pay child support, but he wanted to be able to spend time with his son."

"So he might have a very good alibi for Karl's murder, even if it was one he wasn't ready to tell the world."

Freddie nodded and tension fell from his shoulders. "And if Gary didn't kill Karl, he probably didn't kill Monica either."

"Probably not." I'd like a little more confirmation, but maybe Zeke could find some public record online related to the court hearing. "There was nothing on Gary's computer that indicated he'd ordered sleeping pills online."

Freddie's face brightened. "That's wonderful. Thank you."

I gave Freddie a quick wave and got in my car, eager to return to the museum.

I'd been right in thinking that people were lying to us.

But so far, digging into those lies hadn't gotten us any closer to finding the killer.

If Gary wasn't the killer, who was?

Friday afternoon I contacted Cleo, Alice, and Zeke. After I explained what I'd learned at Gary's office, it took Zeke about five minutes before he texted back, confirming that a court hearing had been held the day of Karl's murder. He couldn't find out what had taken place, but one of the participants had been Gary Boyd.

Which meant it would have been impossible for Gary to kill Karl. Since both victims were killed the same way, most likely he didn't kill Monica either. But we were no closer to knowing who did.

Thankfully, I had one more idea. According to every mystery novel I'd ever read, it was highly likely that the murderer would attend Monica's funeral. One of us needed to be there to see which of our suspects showed up.

Luckily, Alice had worked with Monica on a volunteer project at the hospital and had already been planning to go. I asked her to watch for our four remaining suspects—Gail, Cheryl, Amber, and Dr. Roth—and, if she saw any of them, to see how they acted.

The rest of the day I felt so worn out from the excitement of my sleuthing over lunch that I could barely focus. Plus, I kept worrying that if we didn't find the killer, the homes tour wasn't happening. Serious work like contacting donors was out of the question, and I occupied myself with mindless tasks.

At last I headed home.

The door on Cleo's side of our unattached garage was down, which meant she had beaten me home. Maybe the two of us could order a pizza. I was too tired to think about cooking, and it was so cold and damp that eating out held little appeal.

I climbed out, pulled down my own garage door and—

"Libby!" Cleo yelled from the front corner of the house, then ran closer, splashing through puddles in the yard. "I just got home. Someone's attacked Haunting Harold." Her words poured out. "And they left a note. Come see."

"I bet it was kids." Trying to avoid the mud, I dashed after her as she ran toward the front of the house.

She stopped at the edge of our front porch and pointed to the ghost, who had been cut down from the maple tree and now lay on one of the Adirondack chairs.

Or rather, both of the Adirondack chairs. Harold's head was on the closer chair. His body, the tails of the sheet, lay on the one farther away.

"It wasn't kids," Cleo said. "Look."

I stepped closer. A knife had been stabbed through a piece of paper, then through the white sheet of Harold's body and into the wood. On it was scrawled in large, red script: *Stop investigating the death of Karl Wellston or you're next.*

My knees wobbled, and I grabbed the porch rail for support.

I'd been so worried that Gary might find me in his office. But he wasn't the killer.

And whoever the killer was, they knew where I lived.

Chapter Twenty

I TOOK one more look at the beheaded ghost, shuddered, and drew in a deep breath. "We need to call the cops."

"I'll do it," Cleo said.

"Thank you. Bella needs to go out, but we'll use the back door, and I'll keep her on a leash. The less we contaminate the crime scene on the front porch, the better."

"That makes sense," Cleo said.

I walked around the house and went in through my kitchen door. Thankfully, I saw no indication that anyone had gone inside the house.

Maybe Bella didn't like the icy rain, or maybe she knew how eager I was to go back in and lock the doors, but she did her business quickly and followed me inside.

I wandered into my living room, then heard her bark from in the kitchen.

She stood by the door, still waiting for me to wipe the

mud off her paws, which I'd completely forgotten to do. At least one of us was thinking straight.

I dried her paws, put some dry food in her bowl, then went into the entryway of the house and called up the stairs to Cleo. She came down, still on the phone with the police, and sat beside me on my couch.

Less than five minutes later, Officers Tate and Davis arrived, both of whom I'd met over the summer. If they were surprised I was involved in another crime, they didn't let on.

The police questioned us and collected evidence. After they left, Bella nudged me toward the kitchen and stared at the cabinet where the wet food, her favorite part of dinner, was kept.

I gave her an extra-large portion of her canned food, apologized for forgetting it earlier, and then returned to sit by Cleo on my couch.

"I can't believe Detective Harper went out of town while there was a murder investigation going on." Cleo's jaw was tight.

"Officer Tate said Detective Harper's daughter is getting married this weekend." Personally, I was glad he was out of town. He'd have been furious that I kept investigating the case, even after he told me to stay out of it.

Cleo crossed her arms over her chest. "Well, he should be able to attend his own daughter's wedding, of course, but it doesn't seem like the police are ever going to find Karl and Monica's killer. And look at how little they did here."

"They collected what evidence they could, like the knife

and the note. It's not their fault that any footprints or tire prints have been destroyed by the rain."

"I still don't think they're ever going to solve this case."

Guilt twisted in my stomach. I never should have gotten involved in this investigation. "I'm sorry. This is my fault. You never had people leave threatening notes on the front porch before I moved in here."

Cleo narrowed her eyes as if I'd missed the point. "I'm worried for you, not me. I know self-defense."

And I didn't.

For a second, I considered calling Sam, just to have him come over and tell me everything would be okay, but I didn't. We hadn't talked for days, which wasn't like him. Maybe I'd already bugged him too much when he was having such a busy semester.

And did I really need a man to protect me? To solve this case?

No. I had Cleo and Alice and Zeke to help me. And I was a smart, capable woman.

I sat up taller, squared my shoulders, and looked over at Cleo. "If the police aren't going to solve this, we'll do it ourselves."

The next morning, about an hour after the funeral started, my phone dinged with a text from Alice.

I've found a clue! Let's get together tonight to discuss.

Cleo was working until five, but we arranged to meet at

my house as soon as she could leave the salon. At five fifteen, Cleo and Zeke knocked on my back door, the pizza delivery guy arrived at the front door, and Bella started barking.

I yelled for Cleo to hold on and told Bella to calm down, then I collected the two pizzas at the front door. I dropped them on the kitchen counter and unlocked the back door to let in Cleo and Zeke.

Bella circled them, tail wagging, until Zeke knelt down to scratch her tummy.

"No Alice?" Cleo set a bag with two 2-liters of soda on the kitchen counter and leaned her head into the living room.

"Not yet. She said she'd bring a salad. Let's get everything else ready." I handed Cleo the napkins that had come with the pizza and a stack of plates, and I pulled four glasses out of the cabinet and filled them with ice.

Zeke peered out my living room windows. "There's Alice, turning into the driveway."

I waved to her from my back door, walked out to meet her, and took the large bowl of salad she carried. Once we were inside, I opened the sodas, and we filled our drinks. There was some obligatory petting for Bella and questions from Zeke about the pizza toppings—mushroom with black olive on one and a supreme for the other— but soon we were all seated at my dining table with Bella on the floor near my feet. Alice, Cleo, and I each took a slice of pizza and a large serving of salad. Zeke focused on the pizza, piling three slices of supreme on his plate.

I tasted the mushroom and black olive pizza, smiled with satisfaction at its cheesy goodness, and turned to Alice. "So, what's the clue?"

She wiped her fingers on a napkin and grabbed the purse she'd hooked over the back of the chair. "Just a minute." She dug out her phone and held it out, showing each of us a photo of a small white card surrounded by blossoms.

In big, loopy writing, it read "Thinking of what might have been." It was unsigned.

"Is that from one of the funeral arrangements?" Cleo asked.

"A large, lovely bouquet of roses and lilies," Alice said. "Someone spent a lot of money at the florist."

"And didn't want anyone to know they'd done it." Zeke took an enormous bite of pizza, easily a third of the slice.

"Do you think they saw you taking the photo?" Cleo's face tensed. "After that note they left on our porch..."

Cleo, so fearless when our home had been threatened, seemed far more concerned about Alice's safety.

"No one saw me. I was very sneaky," Alice said.

I wiped my fingers and held my hand out toward Alice. "Can I see that again?"

She placed the phone in my hand.

I peered at the screen. "It looks like a woman's handwriting to me. And not at all like the handwriting on the threatening note. I guess we don't know, though, if that's the person who sent the flowers or simply someone at the shop who filled out the card."

"From the wording, it sounds like someone Monica was in a relationship with." Alice took back her phone and slid it into her purse. "And Gary's flowers were on the casket."

"If he wasn't already dead, the flowers could have been from Karl." Cleo twisted her mouth from side to side, staring at a slice of pizza she held in one hand, then looked up. "Do you think Monica was involved with someone else as well?"

"You'd think one affair at a time would be enough." Disapproval rang in Alice's voice. "But you may be right. Maybe she was cheating on her husband with two different people."

"If there's another person involved in this love triang—I mean—rectangle, they could be the killer." Cleo moved a fallen mushroom slice from her plate to the center of her slice of pizza. "Maybe they didn't know about Monica's affair with Karl, and when they learned of it, they got mad."

"A suspect we haven't even considered." But how could we identify that person? I thought for a moment. Alice and Cleo had a lot of connections in Dogwood Springs, connections that often worked to our advantage. "Do you think the florist would tell us who sent the bouquet?"

Zeke sat up taller. "I-um-na—"

"Don't talk with your mouth full," Cleo said.

Zeke chewed vigorously and swallowed. "I know how we can find out."

"How?" I hadn't considered Zeke. Could he hack the florist's records?

"There's only one florist in town, right? Dogwood Floral?" He looked at Cleo and Alice.

They both nodded.

"I have a friend who works there doing deliveries after school. I bet he can find out who sent those flowers, especially if you tell me more about what they looked like."

"I can do better than that." Alice got her phone back out and showed us a photo of a bouquet of dark pink roses and pink-and-white Stargazer lilies.

"Send me that." Zeke pointed to the image and took another enormous bite of pizza.

"You guys are amazing," I said. "I just know we're going to find the murderer."

Chapter Twenty-One

ZEKE TEXTED CLEO, Alice, and me late Sunday morning. He'd sent the photo to his friend, who remembered the bouquet but not who it was from. The florist shop was closed on Sunday, but Zeke said we should learn more on Monday afternoon.

Not sure what other leads to follow in the meantime, I spent a quiet Sunday filled with laundry, grocery shopping, reading a British murder mystery, brushing Bella, and taking her on a long walk. I texted Sam to update him on the case, and we talked briefly, but he seemed stressed.

The amount of work he was doing for the university didn't really seem fair, given that he was only an adjunct professor. But as he explained, with Professor Brown still recovering, he was the only one who could teach classes on advanced operating systems and kernel architecture, whatever that was.

Anyway, with Sam busy, I had plenty of time to prepare

for the week ahead, even going so far as fixing a big pot of chili that I could eat for dinner Sunday and throughout the week for lunch.

Monday's mail at the museum brought the bill for the new HVAC system. Now, more than ever, I needed to find the murderer, restore life in Dogwood Springs back to normal, and make sure the homes tour could go forward.

Midafternoon, I stopped halfway through writing an email and checked the time. Any minute now the high school would let out, Zeke's friend would drive to the florist, and we'd learn who sent those flowers.

But an hour passed, and I heard nothing from Zeke.

At five, I shut down my computer and sent him a text.

Anything? I asked.

Nada. He replied.

I got my purse out of my bottom desk drawer and slammed the drawer shut. What if Zeke's friend couldn't learn anything? Then what would we do? I really wanted to know who this other person was that Monica might have been involved with.

My frustration lessened as I walked home. It was hard to be completely unhappy going through downtown Dogwood Springs. Tourists wandered the sidewalks, peeking in windows, popping into shops, and looking rested and relaxed after time spent at the slower pace of life in Dogwood Springs. The cozy scent of pumpkin drifted out of the bakery, and the high school band kids took turns filling the air with music at their two cider stands.

If downtown wasn't enough to cheer me up, Bella was

waiting eagerly at my living room window when I arrived home.

I stepped into my apartment and was greeted with leg rubs and a big doggy smile. I let Bella out in the backyard for a few minutes, then sat on the couch with her at my feet, petted the silky fur between her ears, and told her all about my day.

Every bit of tension melted from me. Worry about the homes tour. Worry about the murderer loose in town. Even a nagging sensation that had built in my mind, a worry about whether Sam, like my ex, had lost interest in me. A few minutes with Bella, and it all disappeared.

The homes tour would be a success. Cleo, Alice, Zeke, and I would find the murderer. Things with Sam would work out well as long as I didn't get all stressed and blow things out of proportion. The man was doing two jobs, for heaven's sake.

And just like that, as soon as I stopped fretting, my phone dinged with a text from Zeke to Alice, Cleo, and me.

Zeke: *The flowers were sent by Edward Roth.*

Cleo: *The doctor?*

Zeke: *(A thumb's up emoji.) They were ordered in person. I ran a search online, and he's the only Edward Roth in the area.*

Alice: *So Monica was seeing two doctors in the same practice? That seems, well, rather stupid.*

Cleo: *Risky, but that may have been part of the thrill.*

Me: *I guess I'll have to ask him to find out what was really going on. Maybe I can catch him on his way out to the parking lot again.*

Alice: *Libby! (She added a horrified emoji with huge round eyes.) Confronting someone who's already killed twice is too dangerous.*

Hmmm. She probably was right. I had promised Sam that I'd be careful.

Me: *Okay. I'll come up with another plan.*

I just didn't know what that other plan was. I went into the kitchen, set my phone on the counter, and pulled out the leftover chili. No matter how much I wanted to find the killer, I had to consider my own safety.

When I woke up the next morning, I knew what to do—talk to Kiara. Why hadn't I thought of it sooner?

She had known that Monica and Dr. Wellston were having an affair. Maybe she knew something about Dr. Roth. It was certainly worth asking her and safer than confronting him.

Once it was late enough that I felt sure she'd be awake, I sent her a text and asked if I could stop by after work to ask her a few more questions.

She quickly replied yes, said she'd just bought some locally made apple cider, and suggested that I bring Bella and the three of us sit on the porch.

Tuesday dragged by. Normally, I loved every minute of my job at the museum and was able to compartmentalize my brain into thinking of work at work and murder after hours. This time, though, the homes tour was planned for Saturday, only four days away. Every time I tried to focus on work, I thought of the tour, which, if the killer hadn't been captured by Thursday, I knew we'd have to cancel.

Finally, five o'clock arrived. I slipped out of the museum at two minutes past and scurried home. Could I simply give Bella a snack and feed her dinner after we talked to Kiara?

Well, no. Bella would never let me get away with that. On the other hand, I could count on her to eat quickly. She didn't exactly gulp down her dinner, but it was close.

At last, we were on our way down Elm toward Second, where we turned and walked away from downtown. As soon as we drew close, I spotted Kiara on her front porch.

She stood, waved, and drew one of the plaid blankets closer around her shoulders. It had been less than a week since she and I had sat on her porch before, but the temperature had cooled enough to make the blankets not just nice, but essential.

Bella sniffed at the three orange pumpkins on the hay bale, then led the way up the stairs.

"I've been wondering all day what you wanted to ask me." Kiara looked at Bella as if she was enchanted and petted her. "Please, sit," she said to me. "That mug of cider is for you."

I nestled into the other chair, spread the blanket over my legs, and wrapped my hands around the warm mug. "I wanted to know if you had ever considered Dr. Roth as a possible suspect in Karl Wellston's murder. Or in Monica's."

Her eyes widened.

"Or if you thought that Dr. Roth might have also been seeing Monica." I took a sip, and the spicy flavor exploded on my tongue. "This is fabulous."

Kiara gave me an incredulous stare. "Thanks, it's local. But wow. You think Monica was seeing both of them?" She shook her head. "No. I can't see Dr. Roth being that stupid. It would be professional suicide."

"Are you sure?" I explained about the card on the flowers.

"No. There must have been a mistake in the records at the florist. I can't—" She jerked her head to one side, and her mouth dropped open.

A tingle shot through me. "What?" She'd thought of something, I was certain.

"I just remembered a phone call I overheard one time. I didn't mean to be eavesdropping, really. Dr. Roth didn't know I was there, and at first, I thought it was going to be a quick call, nothing important." She fiddled with her plaid blanket, adjusting it to cover her knees. "By the time I realized it was going to go on and on, and that it wasn't a call I should be hearing, it was too late. So I just sat there, trying not to listen."

"But..."

"Well, you know, when you try not to listen, it's like your ears become more sensitive or something."

"So what did you learn?"

"He was talking to someone named Joe, which was probably his twin brother Joe, who's also a doctor, except he lives in St. Louis. Dr. Roth mentioned someone who had done work at his house that he'd been interested in dating but didn't think it was appropriate if they were technically his employee."

"So maybe he had Monica do decorating work at his house too?"

"I think so. I hadn't put it together until now, but I heard Gail thanking him once for recommending Monica."

The tingle in my chest grew stronger. "So you think once she finished decorating his house, he dated her at the same time as Karl Wellston?"

"No. I think from what he said to his brother, he knew that Karl was going to break up with Monica and he planned to wait a bit and then ask her out. I'm pretty sure that's what he was discussing with his brother. How long to wait before asking her out."

"So if she decorated Dr. Roth's house first, and he was interested in dating her as soon as she wasn't his employee, it kind of sounds like Karl stole her away."

"It does." Kiara took a drink of her cider.

I leaned in. "If Karl did steal her away, and treated her badly, that could have made Dr. Roth angry enough to kill him."

"I don't see it," Kiara said. "Edward Roth doesn't strike me as a killer. And why on earth would he have killed Monica? With Karl out of the way, as long as he could get past the fact that she was married, he could ask Monica out."

I slumped down in my chair. "Drat." She was right. It didn't make sense for Edward Roth to be the killer.

Of course, it could be that we had two murderers on the loose in Dogwood Springs, but that seemed far-fetched. These murders had to be connected.

If I trusted Alice's judgment and ruled out Gail, and if I trusted the evidence I'd found that ruled out Gary and Dr. Roth, that meant the killer had to be Cheryl, Amber, or—on a long shot—Marla the housekeeper.

I thought back to the day of the murder and remembered Gail's neighbor, Linda Owens, coming over as soon as the ambulance arrived. Was it simply a coincidence that she was home at that time? Or did she spend a lot of time at home, and could she possibly have seen something the day of the murder?

It was time to find out.

Chapter Twenty-Two

WEDNESDAY MORNING I woke up determined to talk to Linda.

The first step was to learn more about her, so, once I knew Cleo would be awake, I texted her and Alice. Cleo had never heard of Linda Owens. Alice hadn't met her, but said she'd heard that Linda was new in town, widowed and retired, and hadn't gotten very involved in the community.

All of which made it more likely that she might have been home when Karl was murdered. And more likely that she might be home if I happened to stop by to talk to her.

But, what with a to-do list a mile long at work, and a presentation planned over lunch to a local civic organization, I didn't have time for investigating until after five, when neither Cleo nor Alice was available to go with me. I even texted Zeke, who was also busy.

I thought the murderer was one of my three possible suspects, but I had to consider the fact that Linda had known

Karl. If she was in and out of the Wellstons' house a lot, she might have seen them punch in the keycode, and she might well have had her own reason for hating him and been the killer. She may have come over after Karl's death acting like a concerned neighbor to throw people off her trail. So I had to be careful if I was going alone. On the other hand, I was at least thirty years younger and could probably outrun her. If I stayed on her doorstep, and I went right after work, while it was still light and people would be out and about, it should be safe.

Because of my lunch meeting, I fed Bella when I dashed home about one thirty. I decided she could hold out until five thirty or six for her dinner.

So, as soon as my workday was over, I drove back to Karl and Gail's neighborhood and parked on the street in front of the house next door, a Tudor Revival-style home that was much smaller than Karl and Gail's, but just as nicely kept up.

I scanned the street and spotted a woman three houses down bagging a large pile of leaves in her front yard. Perfect. She had a big job ahead and was close enough to hear me if I screamed.

Was I paranoid? Maybe. But at least I could tell anyone who asked, like Alice or Sam, that I had been careful.

I climbed the concrete steps to the small, uncovered porch, admired the arched doorway and steeply sloping roof, and knocked.

Silence. I hitched my purse higher on my shoulder and then heard footsteps inside.

A moment later the same petite woman with a cap of short, gray hair that I remembered peered out at me through the glass storm door. Her eyes narrowed. "I'm not interested in buying anything."

"I'm not selling anything, Linda. I'm Libby Ballard. We met the day that Karl Wellston passed away." I gestured to the house next door.

Her eyes lit with recognition, but she didn't open the glass storm door.

"I'm hoping you can help me. Gail asked me to try to figure out who killed Karl."

Linda looked me up and down. "Are you with the police?"

"No—"

"Private investigator?"

"No. Just an ordinary citizen, but I am a fairly good amateur detective."

Her lips tightened. "It seems as if you'd be better off sticking to finding lost dogs and the like." She gave an exaggerated shudder. "Two murders in less than a month. And in such a small town."

"Yes, that's why I think it's important that the killer be caught. So we can all feel safe. I wondered, since you live so close, if you happened to see anything the day Dr. Wellston was killed."

Her expression softened. "Well, I do like the idea of the culprit being put behind bars. And I did see something, but I already told the police." She glanced up and off to one side. "I'm not that sure they thought it was important, though…"

"I promise you, whatever information you have, I'll take it seriously."

She opened the glass storm door, and the aroma of roast beef drifted out.

Linda leaned her head closer to mine. "I heard an argument between Karl and a woman. Not Gail. And not the woman who I heard trying to convince him not to tear out his pool. The voice was wrong."

I nodded. All three of my suspects were women.

"I didn't see the person, but I did see a vehicle driving down the street right afterward." Linda twisted her hands. "I mean, I can't say for certain that the person driving was the woman Karl was arguing with, but we don't get that many cars on this street. Mostly the people who live here and delivery trucks a few times a day."

"This is such a nice quiet neighborhood." Elm Street wasn't very busy, but sometimes drivers used it to cut through to downtown. "What kind of car was it?"

"It was a tan sedan, nothing out of the ordinary, except that it had a bumper sticker that said, 'I Heart Cowboys,' with a little heart in the middle."

"Like the Dallas Cowboys?" Maybe we'd been too quick to rule out Marla.

She wrinkled her nose. "I don't think so. Their logo has a star, doesn't it? This made me think of a real cowboy. You know, with a ten-gallon hat and a horse."

Which they had a lot of around Dallas too. "This is great information, Linda. Thank you."

Her chest puffed up, and she tipped her head to one side. "Well, thank you. I hope it helps."

I waved and hurried out to my car. Bella would be eagerly awaiting her dinner. No matter how smart she was, I didn't believe she could tell time. But she did seem to have an internal alarm that went off every day at five.

On the way home, though, I made one quick detour, a very enlightening detour.

As soon as I got home, I fed Bella. Then I called Cleo, Alice, and Zeke.

I knew who the killer was.

At seven that evening, I left Bella happily eating a dog biscuit and walked to the café.

Almost every table was taken, the room buzzing with conversation and the whir of machines making gourmet coffees. After a moment, though, I spotted Alice, dressed in black pants and a gorgeous burgundy sweater, sitting at our favorite table, the one farthest from the door. She waved, and I walked over.

I was just pulling out the chair next to her when Zeke arrived, followed by Cleo.

The server came to our table and Cleo ordered a big mug of hot cocoa with whipped cream on top. "For my suffering," she said. "With a rather difficult client."

Zeke ordered cocoa as well. Alice had decaf coffee, and I ordered hot tea.

Once the server had stepped away, I leaned in and told them about the argument Linda Owens had overheard and the car she'd seen.

"So you think the killer is Marla? The housekeeper?" Zeke propped an elbow on the table and rested his chin on his fist.

"Nope." I pulled my phone out of my purse. "I didn't tell you much about Amber's apartment."

"Just that it's over near the university," Cleo said.

"It was decorated in western theme, with cowhide pillows and deer antlers."

"Oh, I get it. Like cowboys," Alice said.

"Yep." I unlocked my phone and opened the photos. "Look at the car that was parked in front of her unit today."

"The exact same car with the exact same bumper sticker," Zeke said. He opened his mouth to say more but closed it as the server set down our drinks.

Cleo felt her cocoa mug, then used a spoon to scoop up a marshmallow and pop it into her mouth. "She told you she was at home at the time of the murder, didn't she?"

I nestled my tea mug between my hands. "She did. And it wasn't true at all. Plus, when I was in her apartment, I saw a thick textbook about drugs. I bet she could have easily looked up how many sleeping pills it would take to kill someone."

"That's means and opportunity." Alice held out a finger

as she listed each word. "And as for motive, maybe she thought if Karl was dead, she could get back her job."

"That makes sense." Zeke wiped some marshmallow from his upper lip onto his shirt sleeve. "But why would she kill Monica?"

"I don't know." I set my tea mug down. "But I think this evidence is strong enough that I should take it to Detective Harper tomorrow."

The three of them agreed.

Normally, I tried to draw a firm line between the hours I was supposed to be working for the museum and any sleuthing I happened to do.

But Thursday at eight on the dot, I walked into the police station. Even if I got to work late, this conversation would help the museum. If Amber was the killer, and she was arrested, it would mean all of Dogwood Springs could relax. For the museum, it would mean the homes tour could go on as planned.

I gave my name to the officer at the desk, took a seat in one of the uncomfortable plastic chairs in the lobby, and listened to someone I couldn't see complaining about a computer problem.

"Libby?" Detective Harper appeared in the doorway.

I stood and followed him back to his office. Since I'd last been there, he'd added another stuffed, mounted fish to the wall.

"What's on your mind today?" He leaned back in his desk chair and ran a hand over his salt-and-pepper buzz cut, looking quite at ease despite the fact that there was a killer yet to be apprehended.

"I happened to be talking to Gail and Karl Wellstons' neighbor, Linda Owens, yesterday." I omitted the fact that I'd sought her out and previously talked to several other suspects. "She mentioned something that I thought you might find really important."

Detective Harper raised one dark eyebrow.

"She heard a woman, who she was certain was not Gail, arguing with Karl the afternoon he was murdered. Right after that, she saw a tan sedan with an "I Heart Cowboys" bumper sticker driving down the street."

His face grew redder, almost a purplish shade, and he rocked his chair forward with a *thunk*. "Seriously? Even after the killer left that threatening note at your house? You didn't keep out of this? You're lucky you haven't been killed." He gripped the arms of his desk chair and leaned forward. "Let me save you some time. Officers are on their way to arrest Amber Riley as we speak. Another neighbor also heard the argument. At first, she thought Karl was once again arguing with some woman about his pool, but when she saw Amber, she recognized her from her job at the clinic."

A wave of relief washed through me. Miracle of miracles, the police and I were on the same page. "That's wonderful. But what about Monica? Do you think Amber killed her too? I can't come up with a connection between them."

A flicker of smugness flashed in the detective's eyes. "That's because you're not from here. Amber and Gary, Monica's husband, used to be an item, back when they were in high school."

I stared up at the new fish on the wall, putting the pieces together, then looked back at him. "So you think Amber killed both Karl and Monica because Gary was hurt by the affair?"

"Or she killed Karl hoping to get her job back and Monica hoping to get Gary back."

"It has to have been, what, twenty years since she and Gary were in high school?"

Detective Harper spread his hands in front of him in a who-knows gesture. "I've seen stranger reasons for murder. Hopefully, we'll learn more when we question her. The case against her for murdering Karl Wellston is strong. Once she sees that, I think she'll confess to the other murder as well."

"And the case will be solved."

"It will." A calm satisfaction rang in his words.

A niggle of doubt wound through my mind. Was there something we were missing? No, it was just my ego, wishing I'd figured out the mystery first.

Which was foolish, of course. The important thing was that the town would be safe, and the museum tour could go ahead as planned.

I congratulated him, apologized for taking up his time,

and headed to the museum, where I sent a text to Cleo, Alice, Zeke, and—after a moment—Sam, telling them that Amber was the killer and that she was about to be arrested.

Chapter Twenty-Three

THE REST of Thursday was a whirlwind with mountains of last-minute details for the homes tour and not enough staff. Imani had one of her weekly obstetrician appointments late in the day, and Rodney was home all day with the flu, bound and determined to be well by Saturday.

Thankfully, we didn't have any school groups coming in that day, but the publicity about the homes tour, as well as the fact that we had a painting by Clayton Smithton on display, had increased overall interest in the museum. If I had to guess, I'd say the area bed and breakfast owners now had the museum near the top of the sites they recommended to tourists.

Exactly what we wanted, but dealing with a steady stream of visitors, dashing home at lunch to let Bella out, and preparing for the homes tour did keep me busy. Luckily, three of our volunteers, all Alice's friends and very capable women, were helping that day, or I never would have made it through.

At three, though, Bella had an appointment at the vet for her ear. My original plan had been to take her, drop her off back home, and be back in my office by four to make a call to a potential donor. Unfortunately, the vet had an emergency, and although Bella was now fine, we didn't get back to my car until it was almost four.

"Okay, Bella, I have to be in the office to make a call, because I need to reference some data that I don't have on my phone." I reached over to the front passenger seat of my car and patted her back. "You can come with me, but you'll have to be quiet, because the museum is still open for another hour. Can you do that?"

She looked back at me with her tongue hanging out one side of her mouth, the very definition of mellow. As long as squirrels didn't invade the museum, I thought I could count on her not to bark.

One of my favorite ABBA songs came on the oldies station, and I turned it up and sang along as I drove to the museum. The vet said Bella was healed, the killer had been arrested, and the homes tour was on track. That bill for the new HVAC system would be paid next week.

Once I pulled into the parking lot, I checked to see that the coast was clear, then hustled Bella in the back door and up the back steps. As soon as we were inside my office, I shut the door and led her over to a spot behind my desk.

"Good girl, not barking." I rubbed her head. "You lie

down here, and I'll check on the volunteers, then make my call."

The volunteers assured me things were under control. I let them know I'd be in my office on a call with a potential donor.

Unfortunately, what with the homes tour and the murder investigation, my normal organizational skills had been slipping. The number I needed for that call was on a scrap of paper somewhere in my purse.

I sat at my desk, put my enormous tote on my lap, and dug deep inside.

No luck.

Finally, with only two minutes remaining before I needed to make my call, I dumped the contents of my purse on my desk. Wallet, keys, phone, makeup, a notepad, three pens, six receipts, and a charging cable for my phone came out with a clunk. I gave the bag another shake, and the paper with the phone number I needed, a pack of gum, a half-eaten granola bar, my pepper spray, and a collection of what could only be called trash fell out.

Along with a tiny bit of paper that wafted through the air and landed on Bella's nose.

She sneezed, sending the little bit of red-and-white checked paper onto the carpet.

A bit of paper that looked like a piece of the shredded wrapper of candy-apple taffy.

Odd. I didn't ever remember tearing a candy wrapper into little pieces. I was far more likely to fold a wrapper into triangles.

I picked up the little scrap of paper and threw it away.

Then I shoveled everything but the trash back into my purse, restoring some semblance of order, with the most useful items on top. I set the phone number I needed on my desk and dialed.

The call was, as fundraising calls often are, not a one-and-done conversation. The woman didn't jump in with a pledge of money, but she seemed quite interested in the museum, and we scheduled a time when she would stop by for a personal tour. In my experience, if I could get a potential donor in the door and show them how their contribution might be used—and where the donor plaque with their name would be positioned—I had a far better chance of success.

At 4:55, I ran through my checklist for the homes tour one last time and decided the remaining tasks were easily doable tomorrow. I set my big tote on my desk and began packing up for the day, sliding in a file folder with all the details for the homes tour so I could go over it once after dinner.

I thanked the volunteers, watched as they left, and locked the back door behind them.

Then I went upstairs to get Bella. I was sliding on my coat when someone knocked at my office door.

"Sorry to stop by as you're closing up." Cheryl held a stack of papers toward me, one of them an oversized sheet with a drawing of the front lawn of the museum. "I wanted to drop off these plans for the foundational plantings in front of the museum. We can, of course, replace the boxwoods with more boxwoods, but I've got photos and drawings of two other options for you."

"Thank you, Cheryl." I took the papers, glanced down at them, and set them on my desk.

Bella trotted over to Cheryl, sniffing at her navy ballet flats and her long, navy-and-green striped sweater.

Cheryl looked down, and her head jerked back. "Oh, I wasn't expecting a dog."

"This is Bella. She had to go to the vet late this afternoon, and things ran long. I had to bring her with me in order to get back to my office in time for a call. But she's very well behaved, just sitting here in my office, not going down in the display areas." I was babbling.

Really, being ridiculous. I was the director of the museum, and the board was fine with Bella being in my office after hours. I'd never asked them, but I was sure they wouldn't mind if she sat quietly behind my desk for an hour at the end of the day. But I was such a rule follower that I felt guilty.

Cheryl brushed my explanation aside. "Nothing to worry about. I was just surprised." She bent down and scratched Bella's ears.

Bella accepted the petting, then rubbed her nose at the hem of Cheryl's sweater and barked. A tiny square of red-and-white checked paper, exactly like the one I'd found when I dumped out my purse, drifted to the ground.

A piece of a shredded candy-apple taffy wrapper.

Just like the one from my purse.

Just like the ones Cheryl had piled beside her at the bulb sale.

A chill slid down my spine.

Now I understood why I'd had doubts as I left Detective Harper's office. It wasn't that my pride was hurt because he'd solved the mystery first. It was his mention of a neighbor overhearing someone arguing with Karl about his pool.

Because Detective Harper and I were both wrong. Amber wasn't the killer.

Cheryl was.

After Gail and I found Karl's body, I'd spilled my purse, then later scooped everything back up. Unintentionally, I'd scooped up something that hadn't fallen from my purse, a tiny piece of a candy wrapper left by the killer.

Cheryl.

Because how many people in Dogwood Springs ate candy-apple taffy and ripped the wrappers into tiny squares?

Probably not that many.

And when Cleo and I went to the bulb sale, Cheryl had said she told Gail she shouldn't take out the pool, the pool that was probably put in when Cheryl owned the house.

If it was simply her professional opinion as a landscaper that the pool should stay, why would she care enough to tell us?

She wouldn't.

I didn't know why, but Cheryl had killed Karl, and somehow, it was related to the swimming pool.

A warning echoed in my brain: *Must not let on that I know. Must not let on that I know. Must not let on that I know.*

I glanced toward the door. "Thanks for dropping off the landscaping ideas. But I guess we should discuss them another time. I've, uh, got to take Bella home." In spite of my best efforts, my words wobbled.

At the sound of her name, Bella moved to the side of my desk, between Cheryl and me.

And Cheryl's eyes clouded, then narrowed. She stepped closer.

My mouth went dry, and I froze.

She was the killer.

And she knew that I knew.

Chapter Twenty-Four

CHERYL PULLED a gun out of her pocket with one hand and scooped my cell phone off the desk with the other.

I lunged for the receiver of the land line, but she was too quick, stomping on the cord that plugged into the wall on the far side of my desk and ripping out the connection.

And she'd already blocked the door with her body.

Bella gave a low, guttural bark, then charged at Cheryl with her teeth bared.

Cheryl screamed an obscenity and kicked at Bella.

I gasped.

But Bella dodged the blow, planted her feet, and snarled at Cheryl. Her fur stood on end along her spine, her body was rigid, and she looked determined to protect me at any cost.

My heart rate skyrocketed. "Bella, no!" I scrambled forward and grabbed her collar, pulling her back with me behind the desk. It wasn't much protection, but it was all we had. Cheryl had already killed two people. I couldn't bear it if she hurt Bella.

"I hope you never tried to play poker." Cheryl gave me a look of pity. "Your face was far too easy to read. You know I killed Karl and Monica, but you're the only one who's figured it out."

"I'm uh, I'm sure you had a good reason, one the police would understand if you explained it."

"Right." She let out a snort. "I tried to warn you to stay out of this. I stopped by, hoping to learn that you'd finally let this go and were focusing on the museum. But now I'm going to have to kill you too. And since I'll never get you to ingest poison, it's going to be messy."

A cold sweat broke out all over my body. Because her voice was calm, as if she had no qualms about killing me, as if she merely found it an inconvenience. "Don't you, um, don't you think the police will suspect you if people saw you come in the museum and then they find my body here?"

Cheryl shook her head. "With the band kids playing the school fight song and selling cider right outside? No one paid any attention to me."

She was right. My windows were closed, but I could hear the sousaphones creating a deep, rhythmic bassline. Even if I opened my window and yelled, no one would hear me.

Or a gunshot.

She gave a half shrug. "To be on the safe side, once it's dark, I'll move your body. And your car. No one will ever question what happened to you if your car goes down that big ravine near Cedar Creek, catches fire, and burns to a crisp.

My chest grew so tight that I struggled to breathe. How could we be discussing how to dispose of my dead body? I had to figure out a way to escape.

Just like the detectives in the murder mysteries I read, I only had one option. If I could keep her talking, maybe I'd think of something. "The least you can do," I said, "is to tell me why the pool mattered so much to you."

Her eyebrows disappeared under her shaggy bangs. "You figured out that it's related to the pool?"

"Obviously." Even if I had only figured it out a few moments ago.

"I guess it won't hurt to explain. You won't be telling anyone." She adjusted her grip on the gun, keeping it trained on me. "Back when my husband was still alive, before we sold the house to the Wellstons, my younger sister Rhonda was married to a real jerk, a drunk she started seeing right after high school. He abused her emotionally for years and then started hitting her."

Suddenly, I realized where the story might be headed. "No woman should have to endure that."

"No. They shouldn't." Cheryl's jaw stiffened. "One day, after he'd given her a black eye, Rhonda snapped. When he passed out, she picked up a cast iron skillet and whacked him over the head with it. Repeatedly."

"Surely the courts would have understood—"

"Maybe, but Rhonda didn't want to take that chance. She called me an hour later and asked me to help her find a way to dispose of the body. We were putting in the pool at the time and—"

"And you buried the body underneath."

"Yeah. We told everyone her scumbag husband had died out of town, said she was too upset to handle a funeral, and went on with our lives. My husband was on a hunting trip with his brother at the time and never even knew." She glanced off to one side. "For months, I thought someone would figure it out, and we'd both be arrested. But time went by, and everyone forgot about her first husband. A couple of years ago, she married someone else, a decent guy. He has twin fourteen-year-old daughters from his first marriage. Their mom died when they were little, and they've bonded with Rhonda almost like she was their real mom. My baby sister is finally getting the happiness she deserves."

"But you sold the house with the dead body buried under the pool." The Wellstons lived there for two years, never knowing.

"I had to sell it." Cheryl's eyes clouded. "When my husband died"—she shot me a dirty look—"of natural causes if you're wondering, I couldn't afford that big place anymore. I never dreamed Karl and Gail would take out the pool. He seemed so excited about it when they bought the place. And it was fiberglass. It would have lasted another forty years."

"So what happened to change his mind?"

"Monica happened." Cheryl sniffed. "Karl always was full of himself, wanting to act more important than everyone else in town. When he started seeing Monica, he did everything he could to impress her. When she told him there were much nicer pool designs available now, ones that would look better with the house, which I imagine she saw herself living in one day, he was all gung ho to rip out the old pool and put in a new, fancier one."

Ahh. That made sense. "And you couldn't let that happen, because they would have found the remains of your sister's first husband. So you snuck into the Wellstons' home and planted the truffles and the sleeping pills, thinking you'd frame Gail. Did you still have a key from when you owned the house?"

"I didn't keep it on purpose. But when it turned up about a year ago, I just threw it back in the drawer. And it did come in handy."

"But once Karl was dead, why kill Monica?"

"Because Monica had the town convinced she was a big deal. And because Gail was such a spineless mouse." Cheryl rolled her eyes. "After Karl died, even though Gail knew Monica had been seeing him, she trusted Monica's opinion about style issues. And Monica, for some reason, hated that pool. She kept telling Gail that if she wasn't going to replace it before she put the house on the market, she should tear it out and have the backyard landscaped."

"Wouldn't it make more sense to leave the pool alone and let the new homeowner decide what to do with it?"

"Well, yes." Cheryl nodded at me like a rather slow school child who'd finally gotten the right answer. "I tried to convince Gail of that. But she wouldn't listen, not as long as

Monica was around. I thought if I could get rid of her, Gail would listen to me. I know more about landscaping than an interior designer, even if she did work at some fancy firm in Chicago."

"So you killed Monica too, hoping that Gail would take your advice on the pool."

"It was the only choice I had. My sister Rhonda had a horrible life for years. If she had to be separated from her husband and those girls... If they had to see her in prison... I just can't let that happen."

It was a stretch, but in a weird way, I could understand some of Cheryl's reasoning. Her sister must have had a horrible life, being abused by her husband. She might even have been justified in killing him. But for Cheryl to kill two other people to cover up the crime was insane.

How could someone so warped seem so calm? So Zen-like?

I guess in her mind, it was all completely justified. Killing Karl, killing Monica...

And. Killing. Me.

My heart pounded so hard that I could hear it echoing in my head.

If I was going to get out of this situation alive, I had to act now.

Chapter Twenty-Five

I SHOVED the shoebox containing the mystery item off my desk, aiming it at the tops of Cheryl's feet, which were exposed by her ballet flats.

It landed with a *thud*.

Cheryl let out an angry cry and crumpled to the floor.

"Run, Bella!" I shouted as I dashed to the door.

"What was in that box? I think you broke my foot." Cheryl hobbled after us.

A bullet zipped by me on the left, then another on the right.

Bella and I rounded a corner and raced down the stairs.

From the top of the landing, Cheryl screamed out a curse and shot at us again.

But Bella and I burst out the front door of the museum.

We ran toward the kids from the marching band. "Get inside," I yelled, pointing toward the nearby bookshop. "There's a woman in the museum with a gun."

The band kids sprinted toward the shop, and by the time we were inside, one of them had 911 on the line. The bookshop owner hurried the kids, her customers, Bella, and me into a back room, hidden from view.

I sank to the floor, shaky and gasping for breath, while the kids clustered around me, talking in whispers.

Less than a minute later, a siren wailed and drew closer.

I stayed on the floor, still weak.

Bella stood by my side, her body pressed against mine, as if to reassure me that she was there for me.

I wrapped an arm around her. "We figured out who the murderer was, girl. But I never could have done it without you."

Her eyes gleamed, and then she laid her head against my shoulder and snuggled closer.

The next two hours were a blur. The police arrived, Cheryl was captured, and at Detective Harper's request, after dropping Bella at home, I went to the police station to give a full statement.

He listened, made notes, and assured me that Cheryl was headed to jail. I was picking up my purse, thinking we were through, when he stopped me. "You never would have figured it out if Bella hadn't nudged that piece of candy wrapper off Cheryl's sweater?"

"I don't think so. That's what made it click."

"Interesting. Well, her former owner, Don Felding,

always did say she was the smartest dog in town." His eyes narrowed. "One more question. What was the thing in the shoebox that was so heavy?"

"An antique fluting iron."

His forehead crinkled.

"For creating little pleats, like on the flounces of gowns during the late 1800s. You heat the roller and the bottom part on the stove, like an old flat iron. You've seen those, haven't you?"

"Yeah."

"There were different styles, but this one had a corrugated roller and a matching corrugated bed. So once they both were hot, you got the fabric damp, perhaps with a bit of vinegar on it, and you placed the part you wanted ruffled across the bottom plate. Then you rolled the roller across it and, presto, ruffles."

"Or you could use it to disable a killer." He stood and walked with me to the door of his office. "I'm glad it all turned out okay in the end, but I'm sorry she fooled us both, Libby. And"—his forehead creased, and his tone grew more serious—"I know I'm probably wasting my breath here, but in the future, you need to leave the detective work to the police."

"I'm sure Dogwood Springs has had more than its share of murders at this point." I gave him my most reassuring smile. "I imagine everything will be peaceful now." If it wasn't, well, I wasn't making any promises.

"I certainly hope it's peaceful," he muttered as I left.

At the moment, peace was exactly what I needed. Once I

got home, I put on my snuggliest sweats, fixed myself a big mug of tea and a plate of shortbread, and sank onto the couch with Bella at my feet. I was just beginning to relax when there was a knock at my door.

"I bet it's Alice," I told Bella. "She's probably here to check on me."

But it wasn't Alice, it was Sam.

"Libby." Relief flashed across his eyes, and then he pulled me close and kissed the top of my head.

Warmth filled my chest, and the last bits of tension eased from my body. Why had I ever doubted him? I might have been in danger before, but now I was safe and wrapped in Sam's arms.

He took a half step back, his arms still around my waist. "I ran into Alice, and she told me what happened. I was so worried. Why didn't you call me?"

I shifted my weight. "I, uh..." I glanced off to one side. "I don't know. I should have. It's probably all in my imagination, but things between us have felt a little off."

His shoulders sank. "Oh, Libby. I'm sorry. It wasn't your imagination."

All the warm, protected comfort drained from my chest, and I backed away. If he was going to dump me, why had he come here? And why was he telling me this now, when I'd almost been killed?

Aargh. I wanted this discussion over so he would leave. "I, uh, I understand if you don't want to see me anymore." What I didn't understand was why I'd had bad luck two times in a row. But these things happened, right? Just because my ex-husband had grown tired of me, and now Sam wanted to stop seeing me, it didn't mean there was something wrong with me, did it?

Of course it did.

I swallowed back the self-doubt that was welling inside me, determined to hold it together until I was alone.

"Libby, you've got it all wrong." He took my hands and drew me down onto the couch beside him. "I don't want to stop seeing you. I had some stuff I needed to work through."

I flinched backward. "What?" Had he been having problems, and I'd been too busy with the homes tour and the investigation to notice?

He looked away for a second. "I didn't want you to know, but remember when we ate at La Villetta, and at one point you went to the restroom?"

"Yeah," I said slowly. My stomach sank as I remembered how my dad had asked the next day if everything was okay between Sam and me.

"While you were gone, your mom didn't actually say it, but she sort of implied that you were only seeing me because I owned Ashlington, and that if we stayed together, it might be the perfect way for the house to come back into the family.

My mouth fell open. Alternating waves of hot and cold washed through my body, and I tried to speak but only sputtered. Finally, I took Sam's hand. "Absolutely not." How could she say such a thing? "Sam, I am so sorry. My mom speaks before she thinks and ... it's like she has no filter sometimes. You have to believe me. I would never date someone just for a house."

"I know that. I even knew that at the time. And when I played it back in my mind, she didn't exactly say that. But that was the message I heard. And it took me a while to get past it." He pressed his lips into a thin line and glanced away again, then looked back at me. "After what happened back in California, when I almost got married…"

"You almost got married?" I was even more confused. We'd been dating long enough that I would have thought a previous engagement would have come up in conversation.

"Two years ago. I don't really like to talk about it, but I should have told you. And I should go further back, I guess." He slid his hands in his pockets and drew in a deep breath. "Three years ago, I dated a woman named Celeste. I was crazy about her, but she couldn't handle the fact that I worked all the time." He gave a rueful smile. "Rather like this semester, I'm afraid."

I nodded, not sure what to say.

"Celeste and I broke up, and less than a month later, I met Deirdre. She was everything Celeste wasn't—forgiving when I missed dinners we'd planned, understanding about late meetings… There were some issues, but overall, I thought we were a good match."

Deirdre—who he got along so well with—was everything I was not. No one had ever called me easygoing. I like to make a plan and stick with it.

"What I didn't know until a couple of weeks before our wedding was that there was a reason Deirdre was so understanding." His eyes hardened. "She didn't care if I canceled at the last minute. She didn't care at all about me. She only cared about my money."

I inhaled sharply and laid a hand on his arm. "Sam, I'm so sorry. How did you find out?"

"A business colleague tried to tell me something was off. When I didn't listen, he hired a private investigator, a woman who befriended Deirdre and learned the truth."

"How awful." And even worse that he'd learned this right before his wedding.

"In the long run, I was glad I found out. But at the time, I felt like an idiot." He reached over and took my hand. "And I made two vows to myself."

I looked up at him, waiting.

"First, that I wouldn't let work run my life. That's why I sold my company. I mean, I understand things happen and sometimes you have to be flexible, like when Professor Brown had that heart attack. But he's coming back soon, at least part-time. I won't teach a double load forever. If that was required at Grove University all the time, I'd quit. It's not as if I need the money."

Well, no, he didn't. He never needed to work another day in his life. "That makes sense. What was the other vow you made to yourself?"

He winced. "That I wouldn't get taken in by a woman who was using me ever again. So when your mom—"

"Opened her big mouth, it made you wary."

"Wary is a polite way of wording it. Honestly, it terrified me." His eyes met mine. "I really like you, Libby."

Tingles bubbled through my veins. "Oh, Sam, I really like you too. Do you believe me when I say I'm not dating you for Ashlington or your money or ... well, anything other than you?"

"I do. It just took me a while to work through things."

"I can understand that. Trust doesn't come easily for me, either, not after what my ex-husband did." I had glossed over it in the past, but now I explained all that had gone on. How Reggie had gotten involved with a younger woman at the historic home where all three of us worked, divorced me to be with her, and finagled things so that she basically got my job.

"What a creep," Sam said. "He didn't deserve a woman like you. If I ever meet him..." His eyes hardened.

Was it any wonder I liked this guy? I rested a hand on his arm. "Thank you. And thank you for telling me what happened to you."

I was sad that Sam had gone through such an ordeal, but in a weird way, it also made me feel a bit better about myself.

After I left Philadelphia and moved to Dogwood Springs, it seemed as if everyone else had their lives together, but mine was a disaster. But as I'd lived here longer and I'd really gotten to know people, I saw that everyone had something they struggled with. Zeke worrying about the PSAT. Alice regretting she'd never gone to college. Cleo and her high school boyfriend. Oh, I knew all along that no one's life was perfect. But somehow, my own issues had taken up so much of my mental energy that I hadn't thought as much about other people's issues.

And if someone as brilliant as Sam had been fooled and betrayed, maybe I wasn't as big an idiot as I'd thought. Maybe there were just some jerks out there in the world.

Luckily, Sam wasn't one of them.

I simply needed to go forward, trust Sam a little more, and, if I could, find a way to help my friends with their struggles.

Sam squeezed my hand. "I'm sorry I was distant. When I heard what had happened to you, I realized I'd been stupid, and I had to see you."

"No, not stupid. Just cautious." I slid an arm around his waist. "But maybe since we both are, it will be okay."

"Just okay?" He drew me closer into his arms and gazed down at me, his brown eyes filled with tenderness.

A warm tendril wrapped around my heart, and I slid my hands around the back of his neck.

"I think," he said. "It might be a whole lot better than okay."

Then he kissed me, and I had to agree.

Chapter Twenty-Six

FRIDAY NIGHT, my friends and I got together to discuss the case.

Alice, whose husband, Doug, wasn't returning from his business trip until tomorrow, said we should do a potluck, but suggested—since Doug was allergic to dogs and Bella definitely needed to be included— that we do it at my apartment. She volunteered to make the entrée and coordinate what everyone else was bringing. Since I would be busy preparing for the homes tour the next day, she put me in charge of drinks, plates, and silverware. I protested, but she jokingly told me that as president of the museum's board of directors, she couldn't allow me to cook.

As I should have expected, she was right. Despite all the work Imani, Rodney, and I put in earlier preparing for the homes tour, frequent checks of the weather forecast and last-minute crises kept me at the museum until 5:40. I ran by the store for soda and hurried home to let Bella out.

We were just going back inside when Sam called from the front yard.

I walked around the side of the house. "C'mon back. The front door is still locked."

Bella ran to greet him, and he bent down to say hello, holding a plastic grocery bag out of reach when she tried to sniff it. "Sorry, Bella. This isn't for you."

While he was occupied with Bella, I took the opportunity to stare at him, savoring the way his biceps pulled at his shirt sleeves, the slightly messy state of his hair, as if once again he'd run his fingers through it, and the fact that he cared about me.

He stood up and looked at me, as if he wondered why I was staring.

I blinked and realized I had to say something. "What's, uh, what's in the bag?"

"Dessert. It's a new flavor of Minnesota's Pride, Brownie Delight. Chocolate ice cream with chunks of brownies, walnuts, and a few marshmallows. This is the third carton I've bought this week."

"That does sound good." I walked toward my back steps, and Sam met me and kissed me.

Bubbles of happiness swirled through me, and I gazed up at him.

"Now you know why I got here early." He grinned at me. "More time for kissing."

My chest swelled with happiness, and I led him and Bella inside.

Sam volunteered to set the table and put ice in the

glasses while I unlocked the door from the entryway and the door to the outside.

And just in time.

Zeke arrived, carrying a big bag of chips and two flavors of salsa—hot and mild. Cleo came downstairs with her homemade guac and pointed outside, where a repaired Haunting Harold had been rehung from the maple tree.

"I know it's late for Halloween decorations," Cleo said. "But if any of the local kids saw how Harold had been beheaded, I wanted them to know that he was fine. I'll take him down in a day or two."

I peered out the window at the ghost, feeling a little guilty that I hadn't even noticed him when I came home. "He looks as good as new."

"The magic of a sewing machine and a lifetime of craft projects." Cleo opened the door for Alice, who used hot pads to carry in a large pan covered in foil.

I dashed into the kitchen and put hot pads and a serving spoon on my dining table.

Alice greeted everyone and turned to me. "I just got a call back from a handyman. He'll come to the museum next week to repair the walls that were damaged by bullets."

"Thank you so much, Alice." Truly, the best board president and volunteer ever. "But what have you brought? It smells amazing."

"Well, you make those delicious chicken enchiladas. I decided to try making some enchiladas myself." She set the pan down, removed the foil, and pointed. "Half the pan is beef, and the other half is sweet potato and black bean."

"Oh, wow. This looks fabulous, you guys." I gestured to the table, and we all sat down with Alice at one end of the table, me at the other, Sam and Zeke on one side, and Cleo and—although she was lying on the floor—Bella on the other, gnawing on a chew toy that I'd filled with peanut butter.

"This pan is too hot to pass, so why don't you all hand me your plates?" Alice said. "And Libby, can you fill us in? I know the basics of what happened, but I feel like I must have missed some details."

Zeke quickly passed Alice his plate, and the rest of us followed suit, so that she had a stack of plates in front of her, just like my grandfather serving turkey at Thanksgiving when I was a kid.

As Alice filled the plates and we passed them, I walked everyone through last night, starting with when Cheryl came to the museum and ending with how Bella had helped me find the crucial clue.

"Bella, you're a star," Alice said.

Bella perked up at the sound of her name and went around the table, stopping for praise and attention from each person.

After a moment, Zeke tipped his head to one side. "If Amber had nothing to do with Karl's death, why was she at his house the day of the murder?"

"According to Detective Harper, she knew Karl went home early on Tuesdays and Thursdays. She was embarrassed to go back to the office to ask him again for her job, so she went to his house, met him in the yard, and talked to him there. He not only told her he wasn't changing his opinion, he was really rude about it. That's why Linda Owens heard her yelling."

"I have to say, it did seem a little far-fetched that Amber would have killed Monica because she wanted to get back with Gary." Cleo handed me the bowl of guac. "It's been years since she was in high school. She had to be over him by now."

"Mm-hmm." I couldn't help but remember how Cleo had looked after that vet, Bryce, left our house on Halloween. After the homes tour was over, I'd have to ask Sam if he had a friend we could set her up with.

"What about Marla?" Zeke asked.

"Totally innocent," I said.

"She's back from Texas," Alice added. "As soon as the homes tour is over, she'll help Gail pack to move to a new place. For all Karl's faults, he left a sizable life insurance policy for her. And she's decided to have her entire backyard redone before she puts her house on the market. If there's a dead body there, she wants it found."

Sam added more chips to his plate. "That seems smart. The possibility of a body beneath the swimming pool might create problems selling the property."

Zeke nodded in agreement while he crunched a mouthful of chips.

"If it hadn't been for you, Libby, no one would ever have known about Rhonda's first husband being killed," Cleo said. "No matter how horrible a person he was, his parents are probably still alive. They have a right to know what happened to him."

"So both sisters, Cheryl and Rhonda, may end up in jail?" Zeke asked.

I shook my head. "Not necessarily. From what Detective Harper said, it sounds like Rhonda is cooperating with authorities, and her attorney seems to think she has a good case for self-defense, based on battered women's syndrome. Rhonda's first husband was known to be violent."

Cleo gestured with a chip. "I heard that Rhonda feels really bad now about what she did, and even worse about what Cheryl did. Plus, she was the one who bought the truffles from Mimi's. Cheryl asked her to. Rhonda didn't ask why, just figured Cheryl wanted to eat them herself."

"What a mess." Alice blew out a long breath. "But I do know one positive thing. Gail asked me about volunteering at the museum." Alice looked at me. "I think it would be good for her. A step in rebuilding her life."

"You know we'll take any volunteer help we can get." And I was all in favor of someone rebuilding their life after a disaster. From my own experience, I knew it was possible. I loaded a chip with guacamole. "Even if she turns up tomorrow when I'm giving the tours at Ashlington, I'll put her to work. But since her own house is back on the tour, I imagine she'll be there all day."

Alice laughed. "I have a feeling it's going to be an amazing day."

"I hope so. I'm just grateful that you helped me solve the murders. We wouldn't be having the tour with a killer still on the loose." I looked around the table at each of them, the people who had become so very important to me in Dogwood Springs.

Zeke, who was so clever in solving mysteries. Alice, the best board president and volunteer the museum could ever hope for and a dear friend who had connections with half of the town, so valuable in figuring out crimes. Cleo, who knew the other half of the town and was my best friend. Bella, whose love brought so much happiness to my life. And Sam, wonderful Sam, who really cared for me and whose kisses sent tingles all through me.

I'd been in Dogwood Springs less than six months, but already I had friends that felt like family. I had found a home.

The murder was solved. Rodney, Imani, and I had done everything we could to prepare for tomorrow. And I was enjoying a delicious meal, surrounded by friends. I inhaled deeply and savored the evening.

At last, though, everyone left, saying they knew I needed to be rested for the big day.

From the master bedroom of Ashlington, I peeked down at the front lawn, watching for a familiar burgundy SUV.

A few seconds later, the afternoon sun glinted off my parents' car as one of the museum volunteers directed them to park in neat rows in the section of the yard Sam had designated. Even with the trouble my mom had caused, I couldn't wait to see my parents and have them experience the homes tour.

Despite all my worry, the day had turned out dry, the wind was light, and the temperature about sixty. The sky was blue with only a few wispy clouds high above. And, luckily, the previous few days had been dry as well, meaning damage to Sam's lawn from all the cars would be minimal, and no mud would be tracked into Ashlington.

A perfect day for people to see how fascinating local history was and how much learning about it could enrich their lives.

We had five tour groups rotating through five houses. Starting in about fifteen minutes, at one o'clock, I'd be giving five forty-minute tours, one starting at the top of every hour—a very full afternoon, especially since each tour group was filled to the max of thirty people. Already, we'd realized that next year, we'd need to expand the tours to have more groups visiting over two days. We couldn't make the groups larger because of space constraints in some of the homes, but we hoped to have many of the same homes on the tour next year. And we planned to run the event in the summer when we'd attract more tourists.

We had such fascinating tales to share about the previous owners of the five historic homes that I knew the homes tour would be a hit. After Rodney, Imani, and I examined the original blueprints for the Wellston home, we even found that the first-floor room the Wellstons used as a library had originally been built as a music room, one more detail that would allow the tour groups to appreciate the history of the house.

"Libby?" My dad rapped on the open door with mom at his side.

"You're here!" I rushed over and gave them both a big hug. They'd arrived late last night, staying once again at the Hilltop Bed and Breakfast.

"We know you're getting ready to give the first tour, but we just got back from lunch and wanted to say hi. The woman at the front door said it was okay for us to come up."

"Definitely okay." I'd left word with the volunteer at the front door to watch for them and texted her photos so she could easily recognize them. "I'm sorry it's such a busy weekend, but it really means a lot to me that you're attending one of the special events of the museum."

"Oh, we're thrilled to be here." Mom beamed at me. "And we understand that you had to prepare this morning. We'll have plenty of time to catch up this evening and tomorrow before we head back to Ohio."

"It was really nice of Sam to invite your mom and me over this morning for a private tour." Dad's eyes narrowed. "I like him, Libby."

Mom made an awkward motion with her hands. "You know, when you first told me Sam was renovating, I didn't want him in the house, and I didn't want things changed. But now that I see how well it's been handled, I love it. And I'm sorry. I don't think I did a very good job of hiding that I initially disliked him."

My mom was apologizing? That never happened. I hugged her and told her everything was okay.

And she told me how much she now liked Sam.

He'd definitely scored points with my parents in offering them a private tour. He'd texted that he'd shown them every crevice and corner, many areas off limits on the official tour, and answered endless questions from my dad about building materials and from my mom about design choices. "Good thing I paid attention when the interior designer explained it all to me," he'd texted.

In addition, he said Mom had made a point to say that she thought he was a wonderful guy and that she was glad I was dating him—almost as if she realized that she might have insinuated I was dating him for the house. Or as if Dad had told her that was how her comment sounded.

Mom gestured out the window. "All these people paid $35 apiece for the tour?"

"They did." I smiled at her. "More importantly, about half of them became annual members of the museum, which allows them to visit the museum any time over the next twelve months to see our new displays. A few even became lifetime members."

Dad walked toward us and raised one eyebrow. "That's the big money?"

"It is indeed." And with the way some of those new lifetime members were talking, the museum might have some significant donations coming in on top of the lifetime memberships. Donations we could put toward the elevator building fund.

"I have to say, Libby, you certainly seem to be excelling at your new position." Dad squeezed my shoulder. "Your mom and I are really proud of you."

Suddenly, I felt ready to give a thousand tours. "Thanks, Dad. I'm glad you and Mom could be here today." I hugged them both.

"We better go downstairs and join the rest of the group," Mom said. "I'm eager to hear what you share about the place. I know it's silly, since I already saw the house, but I want to watch other people see how gorgeous it is."

"I don't think that's silly at all. Even though our family doesn't live here anymore, we can still be proud of Ashlington."

Mom nodded, and she and Dad went downstairs.

I mentally ran through a couple of points about my ancestors who had built the house and about Great-Great-Grandma Elsie, the former mayor. Then I straightened the pearls that once were hers, which I totally planned to show off, and went downstairs to lead the first tour.

Five hours later, at six o'clock, the last of the stragglers was out the door.

Sam sank into a chair in his entryway and gestured to the matching chair beside him.

I collapsed into it and heaved an enormous sigh. "Oh, my goodness, thank you. I never imagined that you'd greet everyone as they came in and help me with crowd control."

"All part of the service. Besides, it was good for me to get more involved in the community." He winked at me. "And I kind of have a crush on the tour guide."

My heart gave a little flutter, and I reached over, grabbed his hand, and squeezed.

He tipped his head to one side. "So, how did the day go? Any reports from the other houses?"

"It was fabulous. I'm sure you heard how much everyone loved seeing Ashlington, but things went well at all five houses. Mom and Dad texted to tell me how much they enjoyed the day and share comments they'd overheard from delighted people in their tour group. But the last tour group here was the best of all."

"What happened?"

I pulled out a sealed envelope "There was a potential donor I'd been talking with over the past few months, a retired Navy officer. I wasn't sure she was going to donate anything, but before she left today, she handed me this. She said she'd heard we were starting an elevator fund, and told me to put this toward it."

"You haven't opened it?"

"Not yet."

"Well..." Sam elbowed me.

I ripped open the envelope and unfolded the check.

Which was written in the amount of $15,000.

I squealed and hugged Sam. I'd been so disappointed that raising the seed money for the elevator had been delayed. But now, here I was, exactly where I'd hoped to be at the end of the homes tour with $15,000 in seed money for the capital campaign.

I was so very, very fortunate. I had a job I loved in a community that supported the museum, parents who—

even though my mom occasionally needed a bit more of a filter—loved me dearly, the wonderful friends I'd made here in Dogwood Springs, and Sam, a man I cared for deeply who also cared for me. I drew in a deep, happy, breath.

And felt my phone vibrate in my pants pocket.

"Uh-oh." I pulled it out. "I hope there isn't a problem at any of the other houses at the end of the day."

Sam leaned in.

I read the text and let out a delighted laugh, then held it where Sam could see what Imani had written.

Finished giving tours just in time. I thought I felt a twinge before, but I wasn't sure. This last one was stronger. I think I'm in labor. Headed to the hospital.

Epilogue

One week later

"THIS IS JUST A QUICK STOP?" Sam angled his head toward the white, ranch-style house where Imani and her husband, Dale, lived with their new daughter.

"I think it would be rude to stay very long. They're still getting used to the new baby. I only want to see her and drop off this gift." I raised the package I had on my lap, a box that contained a book and a soft plush giraffe exactly like the main character, all wrapped in pink paper with shiny silver rattles on it.

"Okay. I'll go in. As long as I don't have to change any diapers." He made a face. "My sister-in-law was pretty quick to hand that task off to anyone she could. And some of those diapers..."

I laughed. Apparently, his sister-in-law knew exactly which diaper changes to pass off. "I think you'll be safe.

From what Alice said, we might not even get to hold the baby because she sleeps so much."

Alice was right.

Laila was sound asleep in a bassinet in the living room, bundled in a pink blanket like a burrito with only her head exposed. She looked like a miniature Imani, with a head full of dark, curly hair and the same, amazing long eyelashes.

The little one moved slightly and let out a soft grunt as she nestled back in.

I raised a hand to my chest and blinked back tears. "Oh, Imani, she's perfect."

Imani exchanged glances with Dale. "I know," she said quietly. "And she's such a good baby. I was expecting motherhood to be hard, but—"

"But she's a natural," Dale finished.

Imani's eyelashes brushed her cheeks. "Really, I think it's luck. My sister tells me my next one will probably have colic."

"From what my brother said, that sounds about right," Sam said. He looked from Imani to Dale. "Seriously, you have a beautiful daughter."

They both beamed.

Sam continued to stare down at Laila. Despite what he said about diapers, he was clearly charmed.

And seeing the expression on his face...

Attraction rippled through me, and I had to force myself to focus on the conversation.

"Are you sure you're coming back to work after your

maternity leave?" I asked Imani. "She's so cute. I don't know how you can stand to leave her."

"Oh, I'll be back. My sister's got four kids and stays home with them. As soon as I got pregnant, she volunteered to watch the baby for me. Now that she's met Laila, she mentions at least once a day that she can't wait to keep her." Imani laughed softly. "Besides, I love working with you at the museum."

I hugged her. "I love working with you too. And don't forget, Rodney owes us lunch because we figured out that his mystery item was a fluting iron."

"He does indeed," Imani said.

The four of us sat down and, keeping our voices low, chatted while Imani opened the present I'd brought. Then, after more hugs and a promise to visit again soon to see how Laila had grown, I left with Sam.

Sam started up his Tesla. "Ready for me to take you to La Villetta to celebrate the homes tour being such a hit?"

"Ready." I touched his arm. "Although with how much you helped, I feel like I should be taking you out instead."

"How about afterward you buy me a carton of Minnesota's Pride? I promise to share and to make it last at least three days."

"Brownie Delight?"

He nodded eagerly.

"It's a deal." I grinned at him. "Oh, getting back to our other mystery, I asked Rodney about the bank robbery back in 1905. Unfortunately, he didn't know anything more than what we read in the newspaper. But I've had an idea about how we might find out more about Ivy."

"How?"

"I'm going to post on social media from the museum's account, asking people if they have any information that might help us. A bank robbery would have been a big deal. You never know what story someone's grandmother might have told them about what was happening in town at the time."

Sam stopped at a stop sign. "That's brilliant!" He leaned over and gave me a quick kiss.

I gazed at him, my heart full. "Thanks. One way or another, we'll learn more about Ivy. And I bet along the way we have a lot of fun."

Thank you for reading this book!

Are you ready to return to Dogwood Springs for another cozy mystery? Join Libby, Bella, and their friends in the next book in the series, DONORS, DECEPTION & DEATH.

It's not hard to find a family member who wanted to kill the gold-digging third wife. The trick is finding one who didn't.

Libby Ballard, director of the history museum in the small town of Dogwood Springs, Missouri, can't believe her good luck. Cordell Calhoun, the king of spicy fried chicken, is celebrating his 70th birthday by returning to his hometown to donate to several organizations, including the museum.

But tensions run high when Cordell insists on inviting his entire family, including his two ex-wives, their offspring, and his young third wife, Brittany, to the donor reception at the museum. The family dynamic is a ticking time bomb, and it's only a matter of minutes before someone explodes.

Libby's caught in the middle of the family drama but determined to make the event a success. Determined, that is, until Brittany drops dead at the reception.

With the police veering off in the wrong direction and each faction of the family pointing fingers at the other, Libby realizes she needs to step in to solve the mystery, bring the culprit to justice, and clear the museum's name.

But in a situation rife with secrets and deceit, she'll need to tread carefully, or she may become the next victim in a deadly family feud. Join Libby, her golden retriever, and their friends as they try to unmask the killer!

If you like a cozy mystery with a pet who will win your heart, friends who feel like family, and a hint of romance, you'll love DONORS, DECEPTION & DEATH!

Don't miss your free reader bonuses! Join Sally's cozy mystery newsletter to:

- download the Dogwood Springs prequel, BED & BREAKFAST & BURGLARY, available only to newsletter subscribers
- read exclusive bonus content for every book, such as a scene in Bella's point of view
- learn about new releases, and more!

Visit www.sallybayless.com/free-mystery/ to join!

Acknowledgments

I am so very grateful to the many people who helped create this book.

Thank you to fellow authors Susan Anne Mason, Cathryn Brown, and Tammy Doherty, who gave early feedback on plot and storytelling. I can't imagine my writing world without you all there to help me and encourage me!

My fabulous beta readers suggested so many ways to improve this story. Thanks to Debbie Edwards, Ken Edwards, Barbara Hackel, Janice Huwe, Martha Long, Carrie Saunders, and Stephanie Smith. This book is significantly better because of you.

Big thanks to Trish Long of Blossoming Pages Author Services, who edited this book. Your insightful questions made the story so much richer, and you truly are the queen of grammar and style!

Donna Lynn Rogers of DLR Cover Design created the beautiful cover. Donna, you continue to amaze me. Every new cover you design seems better than the last!

Finally, a giant thank-you and hug to my family—my husband, Dave, and our children Michael and Laurel. I am so incredibly blessed to be married to a man who believed in my books even when I didn't and to have a son who is always there to help me with tech questions and a daughter who encourages me and who beta read this book.

If, in spite of help from all of these kind people, errors slipped by, please know that any mistakes are mine alone.

About the Author

After many years away, Sally Bayless lives in her hometown in the Missouri Ozarks. She's married and has two grown children. When not working on her next book, she enjoys reading, BBC mysteries, word puzzles, swimming, and shopping for cute shoes.